ORPHANED FOLLIES

MORTALITY BITES SERIES

RAMY VANCE

KEEP EVOLVING STUDIOS

For my imaginary dog - where are you hiding?

ORPHANED FOLLIES

PART I
A BEGINNING OF SORTS

A long, long time ago ...

My dearest Sonia,

When I told you I loved you more than life, never were truer words spoken. You are my breath, my being, the best part of me. I have relished every moment I was allowed to be your father, and I have considered that role my greatest privilege, my heaviest burden and my purest joy.

Now that our time together has so abruptly ended, I can no longer go on.

Your death has ripped a hole into the very fabric of who I am, one so great not even Oberon himself could mend it. What's more, the abyss created by that hole has driven me mad.

While possessed by this madness, I have done something so horrible it is a blight on life itself.

That is why I must end my life—what little is left without you—and disappear forever.

Yes, what I have done is an atrocity.

Yes, what I have done has made me the monster I am today.

But know that what I have done was out of my love for you, my dearest daughter.

I am sorry I was not wise enough to protect you. I am sorry I was not strong enough to save you. But most of all, I am sorry for the time that was stolen from us.

My only hope is that Ankou the Reaper, who has guided so many of our fallen, will not lay upon you the sins of your father, and that your essence will travel somewhere more pleasant than the place my own soul must now spend eternity.

I love you my darling, my everything.

Your Father

Aelfric's hands tremble as he finishes writing the letter he so desperately wishes he could deliver personally. But how does one deliver a letter to the dead?

One cannot. Not unless they are a being that ushers souls between this world and the next. So from where he stands on the haar-covered shore, Aelfric the Elf King walks over to Ankou the Fae Reaper and hands him his letter.

"Please Ankou, will you deliver this letter to her?" he asks, passing into a mist so thick that Ankou's feet are hidden from the king.

Ankou, as is his way, says nothing. Nor does he offer any gesture, sign or indication that he will do as requested. Instead, he stands perfectly still, watching, once more playing witness to the theatre of life and death.

Aelfric nods in understanding. This is Ankou's way, and through the centuries that Ankou has come to witness death, he has never spoken. Aelfric knows this all too well; the Elf King has stood witness himself while his brethren have fallen under Ankou's impassive gaze. Why should the Elf King expect anything different tonight?

Because tonight is my death, he muses.

And every being that passes from one world to another believes their death to be special, when in truth it is not.

With a heavy heart, Aelfric folds his letter and places it in Ankou's cloak. The Elf King can only hope that Ankou will deliver his final words to his daughter in whatever realm of the dead her soul now rests.

With that task done, Aelfric walks to the lake's edge. As soon as his bare feet touch the water a great kelpie emerges, her massive, horse-like head rising before her king.

Aelfric pats her snout and gives her a gentle kiss on the nose. "Earro'on, my friend, we have seen and done much together."

Earro'on lets out a snort of agreement.

"Do you know why I am here?"

In answer, the kelpie's eyes glisten with great sadness.

"I am sorry to ask this of you, my dear friend, but there is no other way."

The great kelpie draws in a steeling breath. She knows her king's words to be true: There is no other way. Her king must die. But it is more than death. His body must disappear to where no fae guard may watch over him, where no shrine can be erected to worship him, where no reaper may collect his soul so he may rest.

"Thank you, my friend," Aelfric says, removing his blood-stained armor and dropping his weapons to the ground.

Naked, he stands before the kelpie, arms outstretched. "I am ready," the Elf King says.

Earro'on does not hesitate in her duty; she bites down swift and hard on her king's flesh so the pain he feels is minimal. She swallows the two halves that once belonged to her king and friend before giving Ankou a last, mournful glance.

The reaper, as is his way, says and does nothing. His impassive nature is his goodbye.

Earro'on, wishing the reaper could offer her comfort and knowing that he cannot, returns to the depths of her lake.

↔

But Ankou is not as impassive as Earro'on believes. For beneath his cloak, clenched fists betray an anger his kind should not feel.

1

PASSIVE AGGRESSIVE, OVERTLY AGGRESSIVE, NUCLEAR AGGRESSIVE

"*B*ecause I love you." Justin froze as those words came tumbling out of his mouth. He'd never said them before, at least not to me. And the fact that the first time he chose to utter those words happened to be in the middle of a fight was just another thing I was going to put into my *Hold It Against Him* column.

At least those words stopped the yelling, which was better. At first.

Then it got worse. Much worse.

Justin just stared at me as if he was waiting for me to—what? Say it back? *I'm not going to say it back*, I thought. *If I did now, it would be disingenuous. I'd only be saying it because he said it. I'm not going to give in to this peer pressure—I mean boyfriend pressure.*

"I don't want you to say it back. And there's no boyfriend pressure going on here," he said, yelling again.

Shit, I was thinking out loud again. It was a nasty habit I had, airing out loud thoughts meant to be private. I really had to quit that.

At least he was yelling again.

"There *is* boyfriend pressure going on here," I yelled back. "You're pressuring me to spend Christmas with you."

"Well excuse me for wanting to spend the holidays with my girl-friend. It's not like you have anything better to do."

"I do," I said with a little bit too much petulant childishness.

"Really?" He crossed his arms in front of his chest. His manly, magnificent, well-defined chest. Damn, it was hard arguing with someone so cute. "Like what?"

"Like ... like ..." I stuttered.

"That's what I thought," he said with a smirk so self-righteous that his cuteness advantage went out the window.

"Like doing my hair," I said. "Besides, you know it has nothing to do with what I have and don't have to do. I'm not ready."

"For what?"

"To meet your parents, for one thing."

"So you're going to spend Christmas in the dorms, alone, because you don't want to meet my parents? How does that make sense?"

"First of all," I said, raising a very stern and point-making finger, "I won't be alone. Deirdre and Egya will be here too. Secondly,"—I raised another finger on my other hand—"meeting your parents is a big, big step, and I don't know if I'm ready."

Justin winced. I mean, he actually shrank back with his eyes closed, grimacing. All because I didn't want to meet his parents. If he never wanted to meet my parents—well, my mom again, given he's met her already—I'd dance for joy. If he wanted to meet my dad that would be really creepy, because my father has been dead for almost three hundred years.

I will never understand humans and their attachment to parents.

He shrugged and took in a deep breath before moving closer. Grabbing each point-making finger in his hands, he put them together and said, "You've been distant since—"

"I already told you: I get why you proposed, and it's no big deal," I said. And it was true. A few weeks ago, Justin had been cursed and transformed into a very, very, *very* old man. I mean, I-have-minutes-to-live kind of old. Not wanting to die alone, he proposed to me ... and promptly took it back when he reverted to his nineteen-year-old self.

I get it. Really, I do. Besides, I didn't want to get married anyway.

"You know damn well I'm not talking about that," he said, his voice rising. At least he was still holding my hands. "But since we're there, I am referring to that whole incident. Ever since all the stuff that happened, *happened*, you haven't been the same."

"What 'stuff,' exactly?"

He let go of my hands. "Come on, Kat. Don't pretend you don't know what I'm talking about."

"No, I don't. Are you referring to the 'mission' we went on?" I air-quoted the word *mission*. "Where you had one task—to be quiet—and you couldn't even do that right?"

He threw up his arms in disbelief, and given that he was over six feet tall, they hit my ceiling. "I have apologized over and over and over again for that. And besides, nothing happened. That dybbuk demon didn't try anything on me."

"That dybbuk demon—"

"Ester?" he added in an annoying, smug fashion.

"Yes, Ester—because even demons need names—is one evil, evil bitch."

"She's trapped in a box," Justin said.

"I know, but there's a loophole to her containment. She can possess those who know her true name."

"Ester?" he gave me a coy smile.

"Yes, Ester, smart-ass. I should have never told you her name. She could possess you, and—"

"Again, trapped in a box. Besides, it's been weeks."

"She could be waiting for the right moment to—"

"What, suddenly decide to possess me? Or you? You know her name too, after all. Kat, let it go. It's been weeks, and besides, that's not what I'm talking about."

"Then what are you talking about?" I yelled, and my hands pulled at my Dubarry Lily white shirt so hard I actually ripped a button free. *I love this blouse ... he's going to pay for making me hurt it,* I thought in a very healthy, non-passive aggressive way. (OK, maybe in a way so downright aggressive it turned the corner on passive and drove right to the edge of full-on nuclear.)

"I'm talking about how depressed you've been these last weeks. How you spend hours alone in the Others Library archives, always muttering to yourself."

"I'm working on that."

Justin ignored me. "And when you are around, you just mope and refuse to talk."

"I talk."

"You make noises with your mouth, but that's not talking. You're not sharing your feelings. Refusing to admit that ..." he stopped, his eyes darting away like he was about to say something he shouldn't.

"Admit what?" I asked. Now it was my turn to fold my arms over my gorgeous chest.

"Nothing," he said, waving his hand like he was chasing away a bee. "Forget about it."

"No, say it. Like what?"

"I said forget about it."

"What am I, a goldfish? I'm not going to forget about it." I had him in my death stare—a look that has literally stopped an angry mob in its tracks.

"You're not going to let this go, are you?"

I shook my head.

"OK." He sighed, sitting down. "What I'm about to say is going to make you very angry, so please keep in mind that I did it out of love."

"What?" I upgraded my death stare to apocalyptic.

"I know you've been seeing a counselor," he said in a quiet, apologetic tone.

Of all the things I thought he might say, those were the last words I'd expected to hear. I had been seeing a counselor. Went four times, and I hadn't told a soul. Not one single person—especially not him. So the only way he could know was if he followed me.

Until that moment, I had never really understood what a catch-22 was. I mean, I got the concept, but I had never been in one myself.

And yet, standing before my mournful, very afraid boyfriend, I found myself caught up in the middle of a doozy.

On the one hand, I wanted to deny I was seeing a shrink. On the other, I wanted to call him on it. Scream at him for following me, for betraying my trust, for not giving me my space.

It didn't matter that he was right about me feeling depressed. That I walked around feeling as if a part of me was missing, and that no amount of time or sleep or distractions had made those feelings go away for even a few minutes. I felt like I was dragging around a dark cloud, like a ball and chain, while drowning in despair.

OK, I'm mixing my metaphors, so let's just leave it at: I felt like shit. All. The. Time.

And here was a guy who genuinely loved me, and showed it by … what? Stalking me?

I was angry, if anger was the word to describe a volcano of fury trapped in a hurricane of rage.

But given my catch-22, I went another route altogether. "I'm not going to spend Christmas with you," I said in a calm, emotionless voice. I stood up, flattened my silk skirt I bought from a seamstress in China before there were clothing labels, and walked to my dorm door and opened it. "In fact, I'm not going to see you again for the rest of this year."

"Kat, I … I love you," he said, walking toward the door. "I was worried. I am worried. There's nothing I wouldn't do for you, and—"

"If there's nothing you wouldn't do for me, then do this: Go home. Have a nice Christmas with your family. And when you get back, we'll pick up where we left off."

"Which is?" he asked, reluctantly walking out of my room.

"I don't know," I said. "I wish I did, but I don't." And with those oh so sensitive and inspiring words as my goodbye, I closed the door.

2

HEALTHY STALKER
RELATIONSHIPS ARE HARD

I knew I was in trouble when *Legally Blonde* did nothing to lift my spirits. Afterward I lay in bed, my eyes on the ceiling.

A few weeks ago, I was cursed. And not in the fun, colorful, insulting kind of way. I was literally cursed, which in my case meant I was turned into a vampire—again.

Luckily, the curse was lifted less than twenty-four hours later, after I had only bitten two people—both bad guys—and somehow managed to *not* kill anyone.

So all in all, not the worst day of my life. But when the curse was lifted, instead of going back to normal, I felt different. My mood was all over the place: sad, unmotivated, alone, ugly, angry. I felt like I was playing some twisted version of *Wheel of Fortune*.

More like *Wheel of Feeling Like Shit*.

I figured it was just having all that power, only to have it stripped away a second time. That my malaise was a result of feeling sorry for being human—again.

I also thought it would go away. And if not go away, at least become less intense. But it wasn't becoming less anything.

If anything, I felt like I was slowly descending further and further into my own darkness.

Just when I was about to curl up into a ball of self-pity, the earpiece in my purse crackled.

How the hell does he always know to call when I'm at my worst? I thought, and picked up the earpiece.

↔

"Are you spying on me?" I said into the earpiece.

The man with the raspy voice chuckled, his light laughter more like someone trying to hold back a cancerous coughing fit than harmless mirth.

"You know that every sound you make is creepy," I said.

There was a pause before the man rasped, "Sadly, I do."

"It would be less creepy if you just told me who you are."

"We will get to that. I promise."

"You know, I didn't believe Harold the Homicidal Maniac when he said some creepy guy was feeding him information about me. That was my first mistake. My second was picking up this damn communicator when I saw it in Harold's ear. I should have just thrown it away. But noooo, I had to keep it. Curiosity killed the cat. More like boredom killed the *Kat*—as in me. Now if you don't mind, I'm going to go drown myself in a shower and—"

"I am not," he rasped.

"Not what?"

"In answer to your earlier question: I am not spying on you."

"Really?" I said, doubtful. "Then how is it you always manage to call when I'm at my worst?"

"I told you, our souls both occupy the Rooh Ina'ah, the Soul Jar. It senses your distress and communicates it to me. That is how—"

"And I told *you* that I don't believe in the Rooh Ina'ah, or that my soul is missing, or any of the crap you're constantly spewing at me."

"Then why do you always answer my calls?"

He had a point. I didn't know why I did, just like I didn't know why I wasn't trying to track him down or, better yet, why I didn't throw away the earpiece and be rid of him forever. But here I was, dutifully picking up the damn communicator every time it pinged.

"May I hazard a guess?" he said.

"Sure." I plopped myself on my bed.

"Because you and I are uniquely connected. Two humans with no souls. Two—"

"You don't give up, do you?"

"No. And I will not give up until I am whole again."

"So go find the damn thing."

"I cannot."

I sighed. We were about to go through this whole song and dance for the umpteenth time. Mocking his raspy voice, I said, " 'I cannot. The Rooh Ina'ah is hidden, and only someone with the right question in their heart can find the Rooh Ina'ah. The Amulet of Souol is our only hope. If, that is, you hold the right question in your heart. Do you, Katrina Darling? Are you ready to ask the Amulet of Souol the question that burns in both our hearts?' "

There was a pause before a man with an actual raspy voice said, "Well, are you ready to ask the amulet?"

The Amulet of Souol, not that again. A few weeks ago my mother showed up and the two of us spent some quality mother, daughter time finding the damn thing. At the time, I didn't know why my mother wanted it, but I do now … the amulet will answer its wearer one question and one question only. But the catch is that the question it will answer isn't necessarily the one you asked, but rather the question to which your heart most desires an answer. And my raspy stalker wanted me to use the amulet to find my soul.

"Given that I don't believe you, I guess not. But I was thinking about asking it where the best discounts will be on Boxing Day, or—"

"You are not ready, but you will be soon. Until then: Adieu, my fair Katrina. I shall call again when I feel your soul cry out in pain."

"Maybe I don't want you to call. Maybe I'll just destroy this communicator and be done with you."

"You won't," he rasped.

"How do you know?"

"Because we are two soulless humans in need of one another."

"Are we? How about you take your soulless self and—" But before I could blast him with the totally witty retort I had in the chamber, the earpiece crackled into silence.

Great, I thought, throwing the earpiece back in my purse, *I can't even maintain a relationship with my stalker.*

3

IT'S BEGINNING TO FEEL A LOT LIKE CHRISTMAS

*A*ll I wanted was time alone to … what? Wallow in self-pity? Contemplate the nature of my possibly missing soul? Or perhaps remain undistracted as I incessantly worried whether this emptiness would ever be filled?

OK, time alone wasn't the best thing for me right then. Maybe what I needed was a distraction, something to get my mind off things. But given all I was going through, that "something" would have to be pretty all-consuming.

And just as that thought ran through my mind, an answer to my all-consuming desire entered the room: Deirdre, my changeling roommate.

She walked in swooning like a princess in a musical. "I can't believe it," she said with a gleam in her eyes that betrayed unfettered joy.

Good for you, Deirdre. Bitch, I thought before immediately scolding myself. Just because I was depressed didn't make it OK for me to hate my roommate for her ear-to-ear smile, the skip in her step, and the— oh, screw it. I was jealous.

Before my thoughts ran down the path of irreversible rage, she said—or rather, practically sang, "The bestest thing ever is happening."

"Let me guess, Ryan Reynolds has finally agreed to marry you?"

She paused, narrowing her eyes as she assessed my joke. When her changeling brain finally comprehended that I was teasing her, she walked over to her poster of Ryan Reynolds and gently touched his cheek. Good for her—she was finally getting human humor.

"You are right to mock me, milady," Deirdre said. "Ryan Reynolds coming to profess his love would be the bestest thing ever. As a result, I must adjust my statement to: The *second* bestest thing ever is happening."

So much for Deirdre getting human humor, or any kind of humor. "OK," I said, "I'll bite. What is the second bestest thing ever to happen?"

"The FSA is hosting a Christmas event, the—"

"Sorry to interrupt, but did you say 'the FSA?' "

"Yes milady, the FSA—the Fae Students' Association. They are throwing an event to honor the work of Professor Oighrig End. The event will be held at Douglas Hall and shall last from December 23rd until the 26th."

"Three days?"

"Yes."

"And you'll be sleeping there?" I said, really hitting the words *you* and *there* hard. I wasn't going to tell her I thought that was ridiculous. I was going to let my tone do it.

"Yes, if we sleep," she said, oblivious to my admonishing tone.

"Wow," I said, popping my eyes. If she didn't get my tone, I was hoping she'd clue in to my facial expressions.

"I know," she said, mimicking my popping eyes. So much for facial subtlety. "I, too, was disappointed by the brevity of the event. Normally the UnSeelie Court would honor one such as he for three hundred years, not three days. But alas, now that we are all mortal we must truncate our celebrations."

"And this is at Douglas Hall, you said?" It was more a rhetorical question than actually fishing for more information. But alas, Deirdre's conversational deficiencies were not limited to missing humor, tone and facial expressions.

17

"More specifically, A, B and C wings in Douglas Hall. Seems that the dorm has not been able to fill itself since the university started letting in Others. Douglas Hall, as well as some of the other resident dorms, is resorting to other means of earning income."

"Like hosting fae celebrations?"

"Yes, milady. That is exactly right."

"Fae celebrations that will take place over Christmas?" I knew my sarcasm would be lost on her, but didn't care. It wasn't lost on me, and I would relish its sting even if my intended target was oblivious.

"The celebrated birthday of the Human Who Rose Again. It is no winter or summer solace, but still a worthy time to honor one such as Oighrig End."

"I see," I said. Fae and their celebrations … who was I to argue? "And who is Oighrig End, exactly?"

Her eyes widened in disbelief, like I'd just asked who Barack Obama was, or admitted to never having seen Star Wars. Usually I was the one staring at her in disbelief. It was strange being on the receiving end of the indignant eyeballing.

"Why, Oighrig End is only the greatest revisionist historian of our time."

OK, I thought, *not what I expected. A popstar or movie actor, sure. But a historian? And what is a "revisionist historian," anyway?*

I must have spoken my thoughts out loud, because her indignant gaze upgraded to near fainting shock. It was the kind of look I'd give someone if they, in all seriousness, had just told me they thought the Earth was flat, the moon was made of cheese and every story ended with the hero and heroine living happily ever after.

"There are so, so many myths written by humans who have no regard to the suffering of Others caused by their hands. For instance, does anyone care for poor Polyphemus, the cyclops blinded by the cruel and trespassing Odysseus? Or what about the horrible Beowulf and his needless slaughter of Grendel? And lest we forget the—"

"I get it, I get it. Lots of good Others, bad humans, and this Oighrig End is setting the record straight, right?"

"I know not when the record was bent or where it must be set. All

I know is Oighrig End retells these myths from the perspectives of the wronged Others. He is a hero." She placed a hand over her heart, the changeling warrior's salute.

"Right," I said, "he's a storyteller you admire. Kind of like me and my relationship with *Legally Blonde*."

No smile. No hint that she'd even gotten my joke (as lame as it was). Just a serious nod and an audible sigh of relief that *I* was finally getting what *she* was trying to tell me.

"So," I said, sitting on my bed, "the favor."

"*Request*, milady," she said. "And one that will put me even further into your debt. Since I have already sworn my sword arm to you, I shall also bestow upon you my shield arm,"—she lifted her left hand—"my bosom,"—she grabbed her ... well, her goodies—"and my womb," —she touched her belly—"should you grant me this request."

The thing about fae: when they grant you parts of themselves, they mean it. She really did plan to give me full use of her breasts and womb should I request them. "You can keep your boobs and belly," I said. "I'll take the shield arm. Shoot."

I probably should have asked her what she wanted before being so willy-nilly with my request-granting ability.

Deirdre jumped for joy, which for a changeling of her size and power meant she hit our ceiling and cracked one of the tiles. Not that she noticed. She was too busy celebrating to spot all the dust and fibers in her hair.

"The event," she finally said once she'd stopped hopping. "It costs many of the human coins. More than I receive from tending the grounds within the Colosseum—"

"Football stadium."

"I know that you possess more wealth than most."

"I invested in the stock market early, sometime in the early '30s. So yeah, I'm doing OK," I said, and meant it. I had a lot of money, and not just money: antiques, jewels, gold and a couple castles. "How much?"

"We must go to the FSA headquarters to purchase the ticket. And we must hurry before it sells out," she said as she rummaged in her backpack. She pulled out a flyer and began reading, "Three thousand, eight hundred and ten dollars and ninety-two cents."

"Three thousand dollars for a talk?"

"Three thousand, eight hundred and ten dollars and ninety-two cents," Deirdre said, her smile still as bright as ever. From the way she looked at me, I knew there was no way I could get out of this. And when she said, "May we go now to purchase the tickets?" I knew I was sunk.

Oh well, it's only money, I thought, grabbing my purse. "On second thought, Deirdre, I will take your bosom and womb."

4

THE DARK SIDE OF STUDENT ORGANIZERS

AND EVEN THE FAE ARE BUREAUCRATIC

*B*raving a heavy winter snowfall, we walked down to the Others' Society of McGill University, or OSMU for the uninspired short. OSMU was in the basement of the SSMU (same concept, just substitute Students' for Others'), and as we approached the building, I saw that the weirdness had already begun.

McGill was a good university, which meant many of the students who got into the school did so because they stood out in some way. In other words, good universities were where the keeners could finally be kings. McGill was populated by chess club students, fencing club members, school dance organizers, Morris dancing champions ... you know, the crème de la crème of geekdom.

And the SSMU building was the nexus of it all—Sauron's Tower of School Spirit, if you will.

"Barad-dur, rah, rah, rah," I muttered to myself as we walked inside.

The inner bowels of the place were covered in flyers ranging from night walks to blood drives, from spoken word events to beer pong championships.

And those were just the decorations. The halls were also filled with smiling students whose get-go attitude was more than a philosophy they subscribed to ... it was who they were. I remembered passing by places like this when I was a vampire, and could sense who someone was by their smell. The humans inside always had an overwhelming scent of optimism, which for a vampire was akin to drowning in a bowl of potpourri.

Luckily, being human again meant my extra-sensitive nose was no longer so sensitive. Thank the GoneGods for small miracles.

But these halls weren't just filled with overachieving humans—they also held numerous Others predisposed to "doing good." Angels and archangels walked these halls, but that was to be expected. Elves, orthruses, fairies and pixies also did their part, though given that they were all benevolent types, I could have guessed they'd be here, too.

There was the Night Walk group run by minotaurs and centaurs, whose sole purpose was escorting people home. All you had to do was call the number, tell them where you were, and some cloven-footed Other would come galloping to the rescue.

There were public service announcements, like: 'Be careful when at Beaver Lake. Several eyewitnesses claim to have seen the Loch Ness monster there, and we still don't know if it's friendly or not.'

I sighed. *As if Nessie would leave the lochs of Scotland for the ice cold of Montreal.*

On another pillar was an advert for Pixie Cleaners, a group who devoted several hours per week to cleaning student apartments and dorms. All funds earned went promptly to a tree-planting charity.

The Tutoring Society was comprised of sphinx(es), gnomes, qilins and the three Fates—all Others with photographic memories, super-intelligence or (in the case of history studies) who had actually lived through the period of history being tutored.

And let's not forget the hecatoncheires, who used their multiple arms to transcribe and edit term papers for students who preferred dictation over actually putting fingers to keyboards. Again, all monies earned went to local charities.

As my eyes wandered from door to door, I saw signs for student associations, clubs and services all run by Others who were, for lack of a better word, good.

As in, the opposite of evil.

There were no orcs or oni demons, no banshees or wendigoes here, even though I knew this university had many of those kinds of Others enrolled. All the Others who had a reputation for being the "bad guys" weren't here.

This was a pile of poo, if you asked me. So many of the so-called "bad guys" whom I've come across since the gods left were actually beings that were trying to do good, like me. And yet none of them were here, either because they weren't invited or didn't feel welcome.

Either way, it was ... well, I refer you back to my pile of poo comment.

I don't know if it was my bad attitude of late or a bit of my old, judgmental self shining through, but the lack of "bad guys" here really pissed me off.

Not that I said anything to Deirdre. She was a changeling warrior for the UnSeelie Court. To put it in Star Wars terms, my roommate was the fae equivalent of a Sith who fought for the dark side.

If Deirdre was red, she'd be Darth Talon ... but I digress.

Putting aside thoughts of good and evil, we walked into the FSA headquarters, where I prepared to dish out thousands so my little Sith buddy could attend a three-day lecture.

↔

Not that the FSA office was much of an HQ. It was more a single desk, one couch and a few pamphlets advertising outdoor festivities. An elf sat behind the only desk. At least, I think it was an elf.

Not to typecast, but elves are incredibly handsome. Granted, they're short, around five feet tall with pointed ears, but they also have perfect skin, straight, blinding white teeth, eyes you can drown in and hair so naturally lush that full-bodied shampoos actually do more harm than good.

In other words, they tend to be Tom Cruise with pointy ears (which makes me wonder if Tom Cruise is an elf who filed his ears).

This guy, however, was none of those things. His skin was blotchy, his teeth off-white, and as for his hair—this elf wore a wig. And not a good one. A bright orange, off-center, terribly obvious wig.

In fact, his only elvish qualities were Vulcan ears and his less-than-five-foot demeanor.

I guess not every elf can be blessed with beauty, I thought as we approached the desk.

The orange-wigged elf looked up and gave us a sincere, albeit uneven smile. "How may I help you this day?" I noted he gave Deirdre a curt glance before looking in my direction.

Seelie Court snob, I thought—thankfully in my head. "We're here to buy a ticket for the … " I couldn't remember his name, and looked at Deirdre for help.

She was just standing there, gripping the flyer in excitement. "Deirdre," I said, "what's the guy's name?"

"Oh, oh," she said. "Oighrig End." She sang his name. To the tune of *Gummi Bears*.

"Ahh, I see," the orange-wigged elf said. "You do know the event is over three thousand dollars?" he said in that tone upscale shopkeepers use to deter *those without means* from the shop.

"Three thousand, eight hundred and ten dollars and ninety-two cents. Who does that? Ninety-two cents? Ninety-nine—even ninety-seven—I get. But Ninety-two? Why?"

He didn't answer.

"Well, never mind then," I said, plopping my purse on his desk and making sure to flash its Givenchy logo. I pulled out my checkbook and Montblanc StarWalker pen. "Who should I make the check out to?"

"Well, no one, I'm afraid. We're sold out."

Deirdre let out an audible groan.

"Sold out? When was this event first advertised?"

"This morning."

I sincerely doubted it had sold out in less than six hours, and guessed this Seelie Court asshole was just trying to block my friend from attending because she happened to be from the wrong side of the mythical tracks. "Let me get this straight: you're already sold out for an event that is three thousand dollars plus per ticket?"

"Indeed. Oighrig End is a much-respected speaker."

"Apparently he is," I said, "but you do know that under student by-law, the majority of spaces must be reserved for students."

"Ahh, we do," he said in a tone that showed he clearly didn't.

"So if you sold out in a matter of hours, I'm concerned that most of your attendees might not be McGill students. I'd like to see your attendee list, or at the very least, proof that the majority of attendees are students." I placed my hands on my hips in an *I'm not going anywhere until I speak to the manager* way.

I guess being in a grumpy funk wasn't all bad.

He shuffled his arms around, clearly flustered as he tried to think of an excuse to get rid of us. I was waiting, determined not to make it easy for the little bastard, when fate, or destiny or Lady Luck came knocking.

A blind, human-looking girl clutching her purse was guided in by a large black dog that wasn't of any breed I knew or associated with Seeing Eye dogs. The girl was pretty, as you'd expect of a female elf, albeit a bit tall for one. She wore a Mango blouse from last year's collection, trim, stylish black trousers and Cartier sunglasses—I liked her style—and carried a bottle of eighteen-year-old Oban whisky. I liked her taste in liqueur, too.

She was unique for an elf. Then I noticed her blemishes—well, not blemishes, but freckles on her cheeks and nose. As cute as they made her, elves don't have freckles, and I realized she must be a halfling.

"Orange," she said, out of breath, "about tonight's plans ... I fear that Gergeion, Termle and Aileh are—"

"Sarah," Orange said in a harsh tone, "we're not alone. There are a human girl and a changeling in the room with us."

"Oh," she said, putting a hand to her mouth.

"No," I said, still annoyed at the elf whose name was apparently

Orange, "please don't mind us. You were saying something about Gergeion, Termle and Aileh, and tonight's event."

"It's nothing really. I can be such a drama queen," she said, running a trembling hand through her hair, evidently trying to calm herself. "It's just that we have this event—"

"Oighrig End," I offered.

"—and three of our attendees are cancelling last minute."

"Given that you just announced the event this morning, I'd hardly call that 'last minute,'" I said as I made out a check for eleven thousand, four hundred and thirty-two dollars and seventy-six cents. Thank the GoneGods that was Canadian dollars, otherwise I might have had to sell a couple Ming vases to pay for the damn event. "Luckily, my friend and I wish to attend."

"You are attending," Deirdre said, her voice wobbling with gratitude.

"I am," I said, pulling the check free from the booklet. I handed it to Orange. "Consider the last ticket price a donation from my friend here."

And with that, I took Deirdre's arm and escorted my friend—and one of the best people I have ever met in my three hundred years—out of the FSA's headquarters.

5

SHRINKING FROM SHRINKS

"Thank you, milady," Deirdre said as soon as we were outside, "but you didn't have to do that."

"Do what?" I asked, knowing full well what she meant. Deirdre might be a seasoned changeling warrior, but she was pretty naïve and almost always oblivious to what was happening around her. I had hoped she hadn't noticed those Seelie snobs shunning her, but from the way her head hung low in the falling snow, she had. So instead of treating her like a kid that needed sheltering, I said, "They were assholes and deserved it."

But it was more than that for me. After centuries of doing terrible things, I just went nuts when Others—people—anyone—was treated unfairly. I'm sure a shrink would say I had an overdeveloped sense of justice. I think I was just tired of doing wrong, and was overcompensating with right.

Deirdre shook her head. "With all due admiration, milady, I do not agree. Up until the gods left, the Seelie and UnSeelie courts had been at war since the dawn of time. They were right to be suspicious of me, even though I am innocent of any ill intentions."

Good ol' Deirdre ... kind, empathetic and always putting others ahead of herself. That's why I love her, I thought.

"And I love thee," she said, stepping forward and giving me a changeling hug, which basically translated into a spine-cracking embrace worthy of a Swedish masseuse.

In other words, the best kind of hug you can get.

I leaned into it, admitting to myself how badly I needed it. When Deirdre finally let go, I pulled out my phone and was considering calling Justin when I saw a calendar notification.

"Shit," I said, running down the hill, "I totally forgot I have a meeting." Half-turning, I waved to Deirdre. "I'll see you later, OK?"

"Yes, milady," she said, waving back. "I shall look forward to it."

↔

I ran to Student Health Services and, not caring if anyone saw me, into the building. The receptionist saw me coming and just pointed to an open door. "He's waiting."

"I know, and I'm sorry," I said, stopping to catch my breath. "There were these elves, and—"

"Don't tell me," she said. "Tell him."

Looking up, I saw Dr. Tellier lightly tapping his watch.

↔

"I'd ask you what today's excuse is, but I already know: You got into a scuffle with some Otherist and lost track of time."

"Almost," I said, unwrapping my scarf from around my neck. "This time it was with an Other who was being an Otherist to another Other."

"Interesting," he said looking at me over his thin, gold rimmed reading glasses. Dr. Tellier was a mid-aged man, maybe in his mid-forties, with a full head of black hair that was salted with grey. Despite being old, he was rocking a dad-bod, if not a dad-bod plus. He was holding up well in his old age.

Look at me, I thought, if he's old, then I'm positively ancient. I shook my head, returning my focus to the conversation at hand. "It's a whole Seelie-UnSeelie Court thing."

"Ahh, yes. One of the biggest challenges to integrating Others into this new GoneGod World. Humans don't trust Others. Others don't trust humans. And to just complicate an already over-complicated problem, Others don't trust Others."

"I know," I said, peeling off my jacket, "and you'd think that—"

"Katrina, as much as you love exploring this world's inner work-ings, we're here to explore yours," he said. "Any thoughts about what we discussed last time?"

I paused, giving myself a second to shift gears from the crap in the world to the crap in myself. "You mean the whole part about how what I'm feeling is normal and I'm not a freak?"

"Bingo," he said. "This is the age to be having these kinds of feel-ings. Late teens, early twenties. This is the age when people such as yourself feel depressed or anxious. It's not uncommon at all. In fact, *not* having some of these feelings is less likely than having them. We even have a name for it: the Quarter-Life Crisis," he said, giggling at what I assumed was a joke.

Then again, maybe not. Maybe he giggled to bring levity to the fact that I was sitting in a shrink's office, trying to sort out the emptiness I felt.

"Quarter-Life Crisis," I echoed. Given that I was a three-hundred-year-old vampire who had recently been made mortal, I wondered where I was on the lifespan scale. I guessed that, if all went well, I had about seventy years left. So seventy divided by three hundred (sub-tract the one) put me at ... what? Seventy-six percent, give or take.

I wondered what he'd say if he knew I was more likely suffering from the Three-Quarter-Life Crisis, not that I said anything. What-ever diagnosis he was going to give me would have to be done with him *not* knowing that, once upon a time, I had been a vampire.

"Indeed," he said, "this is the age when you're no longer sheltered by your parents, when your fuck-ups—pardon my French—are yours to own with no one to bail you out. No one cares if you succeed or fail. There are no second chances. And amidst all those adjustments, you are asked to know—*know!*—what you want to do with your life. Hardly fair, if you ask me."

"Well, when you put it that way," I said.

"But just because I say everyone goes through some version of this feeling, don't think I'm trivializing it. Not at all—this is very real, and very shitty. Again, pardon my French."

"J'ai entendu pire en francais," I said.

He raised a curious eyebrow.

"I've heard worse in French—in French," I clarified.

At this he gave me a loud, robust laugh. "Clever. Very clever," he said. "I'll have to write that one down for later." Then he actually wrote something in his notebook. Whether it was the words I used or something more along the lines of *This girl is cray cray*, I'll never know.

"OK," I said, "so if most people my age go through this, what's the cure?"

"Ahh, therein lies the rub," he said. "There is no cookie-cutter solu-tion. Everyone has to figure it out for themselves."

I've never wanted to hit someone who was trying to help me so much in my life. That's a wee bit of lie—I've often wanted to hit Egya, but he's a special case.

But still, this guy was annoying me with his *swearing helps me relate to the kids* and his misquotes. So I did what I always do when I'm annoyed: I annoyed back. "There's the rub," I said.

"Excuse me?" He tilted his head in confusion.

" 'There's the rub' is the expression. 'Therein lies the rub' is a misquote. And also, given you're a shrink dealing with quarter-life crises, you may not want to use an expression from a speech about suicide."

Now he narrowed his eyes, not following me at all.

"Your misquote is from *Hamlet*, and the speech is—let me accurately quote it for you: 'To sleep, perchance to dream—ay, there's the rub, for in that sleep of death what dreams may come.' See? Suicide."

"Ahh," he said, putting down his pen and notebook, "but Hamlet didn't kill himself, did he?"

"No, but he did get himself killed." I was annoyed that he wasn't annoyed.

"Hmm, maybe. Then again, maybe he died finally doing what he thought was right." He took off his glasses and bit on one of his glasses' arms in a thoughtful way before saying, "And given he was probably suffering from anxiety himself, when he finally decided what to do—or rather, what he must do—I believe his anxiety would have finally left him. In other words, he found what he needed, and in finding it, he freed himself from what ailed him."

I sighed in frustration. "I don't get it. I'm here for help and you're talking about *Hamlet*."

He *tsked* me. I mean, *actually* tsked me. "We're talking about *Hamlet* because you tried to use my misquote to throw me off."

"I didn't—" I started.

"Ms. Darling … please, if this is going to work, we need to be honest with each other."

You want honesty? How about the honesty of my knuckles cracking your teeth? I thought—thankfully in my head. Out loud, I managed a resigned, "Fine. I was trying to annoy you, but it didn't work, did it? Clearly your annoyance-fu is stronger than mine."

He chuckled and gave a playful bow. "I'll have to remember that one, too. And no, that's not exactly true. Your annoyance-fu is strong within you, but I have an unfair advantage that allows me to win pretty much every sparring match."

"Oh?" I said, lifting an eyebrow. "And what's that?"

"I'm not the one seeking help."

Ahh, of course, I thought. *By admitting I need help, I'm placing myself in a vulnerable position. To use fighting words: I'm the one who's prone.*

"Exactly." He snapped his fingers.

Damn it, my thinking out loud glitch. Getting help is hard enough without inner me complicating things.

6

WALKS, FRIENDS AND PARTY PREP

*E*merging from the Student Health Services building, I wondered how much I was getting out of these talks.

I wasn't ready to be honest with Dr. Tellier about my past as a vampire, nor did I want to tell him about the raspy man and how he thought I was feeling this way because my soul was trapped in some jar held in a secret location only the GoneGods knew where. Not that I believed raspy man.

The trouble was, I didn't disbelieve him, either.

What's wrong with me? I thought, and I heard a familiar voice say, "You're too short, you think you know it all and you're right even when you know you're wrong. But other than that? Nothing, girl."

Without turning, I said, "I'm not in the mood for your bullshit."

"Good thing I'm not a bull."

I pursed my lips and nodded, turning toward him. "I walked right into that one, didn't I?"

"I'm afraid you did. And before you ask: Yes, girl, I have been following you, too. So you can give me all the rage you want now, or we can talk." The tall Ghanaian smiled at me, his teeth whiter than snow. If he wasn't one of my best friends, I'd dye those teeth red with his blood.

33

"OK, let's do the rage part now. 'Too'? How do you know about that?"

"I saw Justin—well, the miserable being that was once Justin. He told me about your fight and his oh so stealthy behavior. Thing is, girl, I've been following you, too. Mostly because I was worried about you. Partly because I'm a bit of a creep."

"Ugh. Look, if you—"

Before I could start in on some tirade I'd probably regret later, Egya stepped in front of me and gave me a deadly serious look. "I followed you, and you didn't know because I didn't want you to know. But I am a hunter with centuries of practice at such things. Justin, as sweet and handsome as he is, could not follow a toddler in a jungle gym without being noticed. And you didn't know. That causes me great concern, Katrina."

"Oh." I realized he was right. I didn't know I'd been followed, and I should have. The only way someone like Justin could have tracked me without my knowing was with a drone or magic, and in both cases, my spidey senses would tingle. And yet when Justin said he was following me, I was totally caught off guard.

" 'Oh' is right, girl," he said. "Now, for all the battles we have fought side by side, for all the laughter we have shared and all the tears both cried and held back, please, tell me what's going on."

It was just like Egya to invoke our entire history together. He was a friend. He and Deirdre were the only real friends I had in this world. Them and Justin, when he wasn't annoying me. And here I was, not telling them a thing, just like I wasn't telling Dr. Tellier anything.

Way to lean into your vulnerability, Kat, I thought—in my head.

"OK," I said, "do you want to know what's happening?"

"Yes, girl. I do."

"I'm sad."

"About what?"

"Everything. Nothing. I don't know, but I'm sad all the time and nothing I can do shakes this feeling of loneliness. Ever since I was turned human I've been sad."

"Turned human when the gods left, or when that curse was lifted a few weeks back?"

I shook my head. Before the gods left I had been a vampire, just as Egya had been a were-hyena. But when the deity bastards packed up and left four years ago, they'd transformed how magic works. Part of that transformation was that Egya and I (and those like us) lost our Other halves. In other words: we were turned human—again.

It took a while, but I eventually got used to being human again. And being transformed into a vampire again, like I was a few weeks ago—even for one day—was enough to throw me off.

But not *this* off. This was something else.

"I think," I said to Egya with a trembling voice, "I think when the curse was lifted my soul didn't find its way back to me." And barely holding back tears like a dam to an overflowing river, I told Egya everything.

↔

"Damn, girl," he said when I finally stopped talking. "When you have a problem, you don't mess around."

"That's me," I said giving him a ta-da gesture.

"So what do we do about it?"

We. Always ready to help, no matter the danger. That's why I love Egya.

"First of all, we don't know that's what's happening to me. We only have a maniac's word. A maniac who, by the way, tried to have me killed. So right now we celebrate Christmas as best we can. Then we hit the books, research as much as we can to see if there's any validity to this weirdo's claims, and if there is, we go looking for my soul. As cheesy as that sounds."

"There is something missing in your plan."

"What?"

"Justin."

I sighed. "I know. I'm just working up the courage to call him— after Christmas. I don't want to get into another fight and ruin his holidays more than I already have."

"Promise, girl?"

"The 26th. Cross my heart."

"Good. Now onto Operation Soul Woman."

"We're giving it a name?"

"Girl, I give everything a name," he said. "I like the plan, but I don't like the timeline."

"It's a few days. Besides, I promised Deirdre," I said, walking away from him. I must have walked ten steps before I turned around and said, "You know, I have an extra ticket if you like."

"Girl," Egya said, pointing at the swollen, gray sky, "do you see what's coming? I'd call you a fool for going to your event in a storm like this, but I know it would change nothing." Egya cackled at this, his dark face almost hidden by the continuous snowfall. "Besides, I got a job."

"Really? What?"

"Snow removal," he said, giggling in that way he did when he was relishing the absurdity of the situation.

↔

Despite the constant snowfall, I made it up the hill without any more stops, forgotten appointments or friends stalking me. I walked down to my room in the basement where Deirdre stood in the hall with two suitcases.

"I packed for you," she said.

"You did what?"

"Packed. Pajamas, underwear with matching bras because you like that, three pairs of pants, four blouses, two sweaters, five pairs of shoes, seven pairs of socks and—"

"A partridge in a pear tree?"

She shook her head. "Your toiletry bag."

"Thorough."

"I had to be, milady. I didn't wish to waste any time. We must go, as the festivities start soon."

"They don't start until tonight. We have hours."

"But given how busy it is bound to be, I want to make sure to claim a good room and front row seats for Oighrig End's lectures. Please, let us hurry." She picked up the two suitcases filled with my stuff and blinked. Rapidly. The fae way of insisting.

"OK, OK," I said, pushing past her and into our room. "Let me just check that you didn't forget anything."

Entering the room, I saw that she had really gone to town on my stuff. My clothes were everywhere. Normally I'd be furious at her disregard for my things, but right now I couldn't be bothered. Instead, I picked up my iPad—the one thing she did forget to pack—and put it in my purse.

It clicked against the earpiece, and I briefly thought about putting that thing in my desk. A vacation isn't a vacation when your stalker can still reach you, after all.

Given that, I left the damn thing behind.

7

LET THE FESTIVITIES BEGIN!

*D*ouglas Hall was the first dorm you saw when walking up the hill to rez. Unlike the other halls, it wasn't a seven-story modern build (well, modern for the '60s), but had more of a Victorian mansion feel to it. Three stories, with a main building in the center and two wings at either side with a snow-filled garden in the middle.

We walked up the central path (which was hard to find, given how much snow had fallen) and through the front doors. There was a small, empty reception, which I guessed meant they weren't ready to receive guests. There was, however, a flyer reading: *Oighrig End: Myth retold from the perspective of mythical creatures.*

We walked into the lecture room, only to find it empty as well. Because Deirdre was so keen on not being late, we arrived early. As in, they weren't even starting to think about setting up early. The room had chairs and tables stacked against the wall. The A/V equipment sat in closed boxes, and there was no podium from which Oighrig End was going to deliver his speech. Presumably that was still in storage, too.

The worst thing about being this early was that registration wasn't even open. Which meant there were no bedrooms for us to retreat to, no seating area where I could unsocially stare at my phone. It was just us in an empty room, waiting for someone to show up.

"Come on, Deirdre," I said, "let's go back home and return in a few hours when they're actually ready to receive us."

"No," Deirdre said, defiantly shaking her head like some young actress who had just gotten off the bus in New York, determined to make it here no matter what.

"What do you mean, 'no'?" I was going to lose this fight with gusto.

"They will be setting up soon," she said. "We can help when they start."

"Deirdre, I don't think they want our help, and even if they did, I didn't pay close to ten thousand dollars to line up chairs and—"

I was just getting into the groove of my tirade when a chair started moving across the room seemingly by itself. From the way it *floated*, it didn't look like it was hovering, or like an Other was moving it telepathically. Rather, it stood at an angle, as if some very small creature was carrying it by one leg.

"Very small creature indeed," I muttered as I walked over to the moving chair and got down on my hands and knees. Close to the ground, I saw what was carrying the chair: an abatwa. It was a fae creature about twice the size of a large black ant, but as strong as a full-grown human.

The abatwa gave me a scowl and said something in a voice so high-pitched I couldn't make out a word of it. The thing about abatwas is, their vocal cords are so small and they speak so quickly that they sound like Alvin the Chipmunk on high speed. But I gathered her meaning from the context. She—no, upon closer examination, I was pretty sure this abatwa was a he—*he* was annoyed that I was in his way.

"Sorry," I said.

The abatwa gave me a nod and continued carrying an item easily a thousand times bigger and heavier than himself into the room. He placed it very carefully down and lined it up before jogging to the wall to do it all over again.

39

"Ahh, Deirdre," I said, admiring how powerful this little guy was, "I think you're right. We should help."

↔

Deirdre and I helped the abatwa move the chairs, and by the time we finished the first two rows, a pair of large speakers came floating in on the backs of two more abatwas.

With the help of the two other tiny Others, we managed to set up the room in a matter of minutes, and before you could say "snap, crackle and pop," we were done.

The five of us sat down on some of the front row chairs. I tried to ask the abatwas what their names were, but I couldn't understand their high-pitched, enthusiastic responses, so doing a wee bit of racial profiling, I dubbed them Snap, Crackle and Pop after the elvish cereal mascots. They didn't seem to mind.

Snap, Crackle and Pop sat on the velvet-covered chair between us as Deirdre pulled out a lemon drop from her purse and, crushing it between her powerful fingers, distributed the crumbs to the gang.

I watched as the three abatwas greedily sucked up the sugar candy, my mind going through my Rolodex of fae facts as they did. Once upon a time I dated a dark elf, so I knew more than most. Still, despite my time in the UnSeelie Court, there were vast holes in my fae general knowledge category.

After a long period of consideration, I turned to Deirdre and asked, "Aren't abatwas from the UnSeelie Court? I mean, the Seelie Court has their tiny folks too, but they're pixies who are usually the size of Barbie dolls, not six-sided dice."

Deirdre nodded, staring down at her kin.

"So," I said, feeling my indignation rising anew, "let me get this straight: the Seelie Court event is run by elves and halflings, but put together by the UnSeelie. As if this world doesn't have enough discrimination—"

" 'Discrimination' is a harsh word, don't you think?"

I turned to see an immaculately dressed man in a three-piece tweed suit. Behind him stood what I can only assume was a valet, given he carried two suitcases matching the man's suit.

"I'm not so sure," I said, standing. Deirdre started to stand with me, but I gave her a gesture that said *this one's mine*, and she plopped herself back into her chair. "I've seen some Seelie Court snobbery going on here."

"The abatwa custodians, for one?" He removed his hat and tweed overcoat and handed them to his valet. He also removed his blazer and unbuttoned his vest. "But consider this: those abatwas need work, and the FSA was kind enough to provide. They could have employed Seelie Court Others, but they did not."

He was down-dressing, giving his valet parts of his outfit as he removed them. The valet, a fae trow whose oversized cap sat in place only by the grace of his oversized ears, took each piece of clothing in turn, folding them neatly over the standing suitcases. The trow's gray skin and sullen look were a sharp contrast to his immaculately kempt suit.

The man finally removed his vest before ceasing his down-dressing, which was a good thing, since all he had left to take off were his shirt, pants and gloves. Then again, he was quite attractive, so maybe it wasn't a good thing after all.

I had expected him to take off his gloves, but he kept those on, an odd contrast with his white, pearl button dress shirt and crisp black trousers.

"So I suppose it's because of some kind of equal opportunity scheme that you have a trow valet?"

"You mean Jarvis here?" He patted the trow on the shoulder. "This UnSeelie Court creature is not just my valet—he is my friend. A friend, mind you, with whom I have shared many a wild adventure. Isn't that true, my ol' buddy, you?" The man giggled as he spoke.

The trow did not.

"Evidently." I decided not to continue down this path, which would only lead to a fight. I'd be stuck with this guy for three days—plenty of time to fight him over Christmas dinner. So I changed tact. "You're not fae, are you?"

He snapped his feet together and gave me a playful salute. " 'Fraid not, ma'am. A fae enthusiast, yes, but my fruit blooms on the homo sapien branch of the tree of life."

"Humph," I said, not returning his salute. "You dress like an elf." I forced an *I'm kidding, but really I'm not* smile.

"I like to think I dress like an aged professor the university can't remove because I have tenure."

"But you're not a professor."

"No."

"Soldier?"

"Very good," he said. "What gave me away?"

"Your cute salute was a bit too proper and practiced for someone who's never served."

"Really?" He drew in close to me. "Tell me more."

He extended his hand, and up close (and with me less blinded by rage) I noticed that this guy was really cute. More than cute: handsome in a boyish way. And I would have mistaken him for a person of privilege and pampering if it wasn't for his eyes. They carried a sadness in them only born of truly losing something you love.

"OK," I said, "for one thing, your forearm was at a 45-degree angle while your upper arm was parallel to the ground. For another, your posture was too straight, and … well, all of it, really. The only thing that didn't scream military was the goofy smile you gave me. That, and the fact that you obviously have money. Lots of it."

"Born into the money, chose the military life partly because—"

"You want to go into politics."

"I want to go into politics. That is why I joined. But I *chose* the military life because once I got a taste of duty and honor … well, principles can be addictive."

"Humph," I said.

"So a goofy smile, eh? I was going for cute and approachable."

I rolled my eyes. "Mission failed."

"Seems so." He extended his hand. "I'm Remi LeChance. Canadian Armed Forces and, as I mentioned earlier, fae enthusiast."

I took his hand. "Don't forget rich." I nodded at his valet.

"Like you aren't. With a three-thousand-dollar ticket price, I think we're all people of privilege, are we not?" He spoke to the room, which consisted of Deirdre, three abatwas, his valet and me.

"Read the room, buddy," I said.

He looked around and his cheeks turned a rosy red. "Ahh, yes. My apologies."

8

SNOWED-IN SPEECHES AND CONFINED TENSIONS

*O*ver the next hour, two more guests showed up. The first was an eleven-foot giant who wore jeans that must have been XXXXXXL (where you could buy one of those, I had no idea) and a moo-moo stretched across his ample chest. The huge fae creature had long blond hair and wore something around his neck that, given his height, I couldn't quite make out. The second guest was an elf dressed in a black suit so conservative it was only really appropriate for a funeral. Neither spoke as they entered the room, and from the casual way they greeted Remi, I doubted they knew each other.

Great, I thought, *five guests, four non-attendees, no host and no speaker*. And just as I was getting ready to vocalize the rare thought I didn't say out loud, in walked Orange wearing his uneven smile and carrying a box full of keys.

"Hello everyone," he said, trying to clap while carrying the box. Instead of his palms making attention-grabbing noise, the keys in the box jiggled and clacked against one another, gathering our attention all the same. "I have keys, keys, keys."

Everyone in the room stood up and Orange pulled out a key. "Freol Garfum," Orange said, and the elf who looked like he was attending a funeral stood up. "You're on the third floor. OK, next. Jack ... ahh, just Jack," he said. The giant stepped forward and took the key. "You're on the ground floor. Taller ceiling here." Orange pointed up.

Jack grunted his approval, and as the giant hunched away from Orange, I wondered if anyone had ever told Jack that his name was usually reserved for the guy who kills the giant—not the giant himself.

"Remi LaChance," Orange practically sang as he pulled out two keys. Jarvis the valet stepped forward, and as Orange passed the keys to him, I swore that Jarvis's hand lingered a little too long for such a simple task.

"And saving the best for last," he said in a lackluster voice, "Katrina and Deirdre Darling." He tossed us a key each. "You're both on the second floor."

"First of all, it's Katrina Darling and Deirdre Goodforest. We're not together. Well, we are together, it's just we're not *together*, together. Not that being together is a problem ..." I stumbled over myself. "I mean, we need two separate rooms."

"Two rooms?" He looked at the printout he'd brought. "I have you down for one."

"And I paid for three."

Orange paused for a second as he decided whether it was worth his time to get into another argument with me before huffing and pulling out the last set of keys from his box. "Fine, here you go." He tossed them to me.

Free of the box of keys, he successfully clapped his hands this time. "So, good news and bad, I'm afraid. The good is Oighrig End is here. I have seen him to his room and he is settling in. You will all get to meet him at 5pm, when he will deliver a short introductory lecture, after which we will retire to the dining hall for dinner and drinks."

Everyone nodded in approval, and Deirdre, bless her, actually clapped with glee. Orange stood there surveying us for a long, awkward second before I said, "And the bad news?"

"Ahh yes," he said. "I fear we are the only ones who will be in attendance. Many have cancelled because of the snowstorm. Seems our three friends from the north couldn't manage the treacherous roads to be with us today." As he spoke, his focus seemed to be solely on Remi. "Regardless, we shall have a great festivity. So go, prepare. Oighrig End will be with us soon!"

With that said, he pointed at the door—the universal gesture for *get out*.

9

MEETING YOUR HEROES SUCKS

*D*eirdre and I dressed for the lecture. I chose to wear a cute little number I'd bought from Goddiva, while Deirdre wore a simple tank top, miniskirt and fishnet stockings. I would have made a comment about corners and *looking for a good time*, except she accessorized her outfit with camellias, magnolias and freesias.

By the time she was done, she looked less street-walkerish and more child-of-the-Earthish. Her outfit was gorgeous, her smile was radiant and she was perfect.

Compared to her, I was a sow. A sow in a very expensive, very stylish outfit.

"Ready?" I said, looking out the window at the continuous snow-fall. It was looking pretty ominous out there.

"How can one ever be ready to meet their hero?" She offered me her hand.

Taking it, the two of us walked downstairs to what I was sure was going to be an extremely boring lecture.

For me, at least.

↔

. . .

The lecture hall was designed for about forty people, and given that it was literally just Deirdre, Remi, Freol, Jack and me, the room felt empty. Not that that deterred Orange's enthusiasm any. He clapped as we entered, gesturing for us all to sit at the front of the room.

Jack the giant sat in the center, which was a good thing. His massive stature blocked anyone on the stage from actually seeing how empty the room was. Thank the GoneGods for big giants and small miracles.

With us seated, Orange skipped to a side door and opened it. The blind girl from earlier, guided by her black dog, walked in and made her way to the stage. Once she was seated, she turned her head toward us, giving us more of her left ear than her eyes. "Today we have the rare and long overdue pleasure of righting great wrongs once done. Too long have myths been told with human bias, and with the help of our guest of honor, we will be able to set the record straight. But you don't want to hear that from me, do you?"

Remi cupped his hand over his mouth and said in an exaggerated tone, "Bring out the End."

Laughter sounded around the room as Sarah smiled. "Very well, then. Without further ado, I present to you: Oighrig End."

Everyone clapped as a balding man with a terrible comb over, an outdated tweed blazer and black jeans walked onto the stage. Based on how loudly Deirdre clapped, I could only assume that was Oighrig End.

↔

Oighrig End sat on the other chair, and from the coy smile he wore, I could tell he was basking in the applause. I could also tell from how he scanned the empty room that he was disappointed to be performing for such a small audience.

Once the adulation died away (which boiled down to the moment Deirdre stopped clapping, as the others had stopped as soon as he'd been seated), he raised a hand and said, "Ciamar a tha a h-uile duine?"

Humph. Scottish Gaelic for "How is everyone doing?" Granted, my homeland was a hotspot for fae activity, but it was still strange he didn't say it in Elvish.

The audience, however, didn't find it strange because they all laughed, responding with "Iontach." I guessed I missed some inside joke.

Deirdre, seeing that I wasn't laughing, leaned in close and said in an exuberant whisper, loud enough for everyone to hear, "It means 'wonderful' in Irish. It is funny because he is using the mortal dialects of the lands from which we hail. Very clever, don't you think?"

"Yes," I whispered, wondering if everyone could also hear my cheeks boiling over into a blush. "Now shush."

Oighrig End gave me a curious look. "A new fan, I see. Human, too. How rare."

"Not that rare," Remi said, and there was more laughter.

"Indeed. First of all, welcome, and thank you for braving this terrible storm. I hear we're expecting another ten inches this evening. I hope the true guest of honor arrived unimpeded ... the goose."

More laughter. When I didn't laugh again, Deirdre whisper-shouted, "Goose is the traditional celebratory bird from the United Kingdom. It shall be our meal tonight."

"First of all," I whispered back, "I know. I'm Scottish. Secondly, please stop explaining things to me."

"Oh," Oighrig End said, pointing at Deirdre, "I don't know if you need be so shy, dear. This is an intimate setting, and the cradle-robber is only helping."

At the words "cradle-robber," everyone chuckled. Everyone except Deirdre and me, who kept our mouths shut. This time Deirdre didn't try to explain the joke—not that I needed her to. Changelings were famous for infiltrating enemy camps by kidnapping children and using magic to change their appearance to look like the child they'd taken.

Deirdre's non-reaction meant his distasteful joke had hurt her feelings. Deirdre might once have been a powerful warrior for the UnSeelie Court, but now she was a kind, gentle creature who could no more hurt an ant than a child.

The only consolation prize for Oighrig End's joke was that the other fae only gave him a polite chuckle, evidently not finding the joke funny, either.

I mentally assigned a *strike one* in Oighrig End's column.

If Oighrig End thought his joke was distasteful, he made no show of it. Instead, he pulled out some cue cards from his inner jacket pocket and said, "Long has it been that history has been written by humans. And, as sad and confusing as the gods' departure may be, one boon has come from their absence: We finally get a chance to set the record straight."

At this, everyone clapped. Even Deirdre, her exuberance returned. Evidently she had forgiven this man much faster than I could.

That was part of what made her so wonderful.

"How sneaky it is of us humans"—Oighrig put a hand on his chest —"to praise the conniving miller's daughter when she snuck into Rumpelstiltskin's home to steal his name. What of Hansel and Gretel, and how they burned the poor witch to death after trespassing onto her lands? And don't even get me started on that bitch Little Red Riding Hood ..."

Everyone laughed, and even though I didn't find that comment funny (after all, wasn't Little Red Riding Hood just defending herself? And how often did I play wolf when I was a vampire?), I forced a fake laugh. Deirdre nodded approvingly.

"And so, in an effort to apologize for my species' unfairness, I humbly offer my services to the Other communities, choosing to examine these stories and tell them as they truly happened."

He paused expectantly, waiting for more claps, and much to my surprise, the only one who did was Deirdre. Everyone else was surprisingly quiet. More pointedly, Sarah, who had been smiling earlier, pursed her lips in displeasure. I had no idea what had upset the halfling, and from the way Deirdre behaved, neither did she.

This rattled Oighrig End, who flipped through some cue cards before saying, "Ahh, yes … the latest myth I am exploring is that of Sinbad and the horrid crime he committed against—"

"Arabian mythology," Remi interrupted. "If you don't mind, we are all fae or friends of fae here. Can we hear those stories instead?"

Oighrig End's eyes widened before he nodded. "I haven't prepared, and I fear my memory isn't what it once was, but if you are willing to indulge a few plot holes, as it were, then yes. Which story or stories did you have in mind?"

"Let us aim high. Tell us of the Red Cross Knight and his escapades within the annals of Spencer's *Faerie Queen*." There were several nods, and Jack the giant put his hands together in what sounded more like thunder than claps.

"Indeed, one of the most famous stories. Which part shall we explore?"

"Well," Sarah cut in, "since we're talking about *The Faerie Queen*, I was curious about Archimago. He was a human, I believe."

"He was indeed," Oighrig End said. "A sorcerer of such infamy and trickery that it is quite literally a crime he is no longer with us so that we may not bestow modern justice on him."

"Hear, hear," Orange said.

I looked over at Deirdre, who solemnly nodded in agreement. This Archimago was one evil human sorcerer, and even though every wrong he did to the fae world was centuries ago, I guess they all still held a grudge.

"He was one of the few humans who could freely travel the human world, as well as the lands of the Seelie and UnSeelie Courts," Oighrig End said.

"And he was a rabble rouser who tried to start a war between the fae and human worlds," Remi added.

"Ahh," Oighrig End said, wagging a finger in a condescending manner, "indeed he did. Both humans and fae wrote this, but I fear both may have gotten it wrong. Understandable, really: among the handful of traits fae and humans share, bias is one of them," he said, arrogantly looking at his nails. "I propose that Archimago is a far more complex character than how he is portrayed in myth and history. A unifying force who wanted to marry the two worlds, not divide them."

"That sounds like a myth, my dear Professor End," Remi said, to the delight of the others.

"Perhaps, but I will make the argument nonetheless in my latest book." He set a hand by his mouth and said in a stage whisper, "Shameless book plug."

No one laughed, and an awkward silence filled the room. Sarah cleared her throat. "Speaking of dividing worlds, I often wondered about Archimago and his role in King Orfeo's story. After all, the fae version tells a different story than the human one."

Oighrig End clapped his hands. "That is a myth I hold dear to my heart. In it, King Orfeo traversed the lands of the UnSeelie Court to rescue his wife Heurodis from the evil Elf King, who had kidnapped her."

"Evil?" Sarah said.

"Well, that is the human interpretation. But one can see their point: the Elf King did lure Orfeo's wife away from the mortal lands. From Orfeo's perspective, he kidnapped her. A vile act."

"No," Deirdre said, "they were in love."

"Ahh yes, that is what the UnSeelie Court historian would have you believe. I, on the other hand, have interviewed many on the subject, and it seems this is one case where the humans got it right: the Elf King *did* kidnap Orfeo's wife Heurodis. And King Orfeo did risk all to win her back. As for your comment, Sarah, in all the pages written by human or fae, there is no mention of Archimago."

"True, but I believe this might be an oversight. After all, it is not easy for a human to enter the fae world. King Orfeo must have been a sorcerer in his own right to be able to even enter the Elf King's lands."

"Good point, young lady," Remi chimed in. "We know this legend to be true … parts of it, at least. How could a human enter the UnSeelie Court if not by his own power, or perhaps the power of another such as Archimago? As I see it, either King Orfeo was Archimago, or Archimago helped him enter to cause strife between the two worlds. I don't suppose you have any insight into the myth? Or perhaps you never considered this before." Now it was Remi's turn to be condescending.

"Well, I …" Oighrig End's face reddened as he flipped through his notes. He was visibly flustered by Remi's and Sarah's questions, but there was something more than annoyance in his demeanor. He was also angry. Perhaps at himself, for not knowing the answer. Or perhaps at them, for challenging him. Either way, the human professor did little to hide his frustration.

Orange, sensing the shift in mood, walked to the stage. "Now, now, let's not press our guest. As knowledgeable as he is, he certainly can't know all the answers."

"Actually," Oighrig said, waving Orange away, "I have investigated this one in great detail."

"You have?" the ugly elf said, clearly impressed by the human revisionist historian.

"I have. In fact, this very myth features heavily in my next book. To answer Remi's question, all my research indicates two things. One,"— he held up a finger in Remi's direction—"King Orfeo's love for Heurodis was so complete that his heart acted as a compass—or perhaps the better word is a magnet—that guided him to her. Two, when his heart found the border between the UnSeelie Court and the mortal realm, a goblin by the name of Redcap, aided by his trow lover, let the human king in. Why? No one is sure, other than to say that goblins and trow are evil little buggers. Are they not?"

He pointed at Jarvis. I've met trows before—they have an unhealthy temper. Well, unhealthy for the person they're angry at. But much to this trow's credit, he didn't react. He simply stared at the professor with calm, even eyes.

Oighrig End sighed. "I fear, my fae brethren, that this is one instance where human history got it right. The Elf King really did kidnap Orfeo's wife, and the human king really did risk much to save his love."

"But—" started Sarah.

"I know, I know," Oighrig End said. "The UnSeelie Court would have you believe that the Elf King loved Heurodis, and that it was King Orfeo who wronged the Elf King by sneaking into his lands and kidnapping her. But the thing about the fae of the UnSeelie Court is: they like to play the victim, and have no qualms about lying. My research, and the inconsistent interviews I have had with several UnSeelie Court members who were part of the Elf King's court, tells me that the humans got it right.

"Furthermore, the myth of King Orfeo and the Elf King does not end there. It seems that the Elf King was so angered by King Orfeo's insult—not that *un*kidnapping one's wife should be taken as an insult —that he single-handedly attacked King Orfeo's castle. Legend says he wiped out every last man, woman and child residing there before facing off against the human king. There was a great sword fight between them, and in the end, King Orfeo dispatched the Elf King with a mighty blow, felling the Elf King before dying from his own wounds." Oighrig End swung an imaginary sword as he spoke.

"But alas," Professor End continued after his little air battle had ended, "that is the legend. Most likely the Elf King was exhausted, perhaps wounded after having literally taken down a human army by himself, and King Orfeo was easy prey." Oighrig looked around at the audience who, if they were enjoying this lecture, didn't really make any indication one way or another.

Oighrig End, unfazed by their lack of reaction, smiled. "Again, this will all be in my next book. I do hope you will all purchase it. And tweet about it. Can't have a successful book in this day and age without digital birds tweeting its praise."

10

FESTIVITIES? I'D RATHER SLEEP

I was right about one thing: the rest of the talk did turn into a boring lecture about fae, myths and revisions. I did everything in my power not to fall asleep, and I was so not listening that I didn't even realize when it was over.

Luckily, everyone stood up to shake Oighrig End's hand, and I took it as my cue to do the same.

Orange jumped on the stage and said in his overexcited way, "OK, time to retire for a quick rest before dinner. See you all at eight. And a word of caution: seems the storm has gotten worse, so no going outside. We have enough food to survive for a fortnight, so stay indoors. Stay safe."

I didn't need to be told twice, and was already at the door before he said "eight." I turned to see where Deirdre was—at the front, shaking Oighrig's hand—and opting not to wait for her, I decided to go upstairs ... but not before I saw Jack giving me one hell of a dirty look.

He probably saw how uninterested I was in the whole thing. Ignoring the giant, I went to my room.

↔

An hour later, Deirdre walked in my room and I could see the mixed look of adulation and grief. She had met her hero, and he had insulted her. What's more, he had insulted her kind when he said that members of the UnSeelie Court were seasoned liars.

This is why you should never meet your heroes.

"Dinner is in a few minutes," she said in a deflated voice.

"I know," I said. "I think I'm going to sit this one out."

She nodded, and instead of arguing with me as I expected, she turned toward the door.

"Deirdre," I called after her.

She paused at my door's threshold.

"Did you know the Elf King?"

She shook her head. "He ruled over one of the UnSeelie Court kingdoms, but not mine. Still, his story is well known, and although he was not my king, I would have gladly travelled to his lands to fight by his side, to aid him in conquering the mortal realms. That was how terrible the human's crime was."

"But you didn't," I said. "Why?"

"Because in the end, the dark elf was a wise king. He would not let his desire for revenge draw legions of fae into war. He faced his enemies alone ... and perished."

"Like Oighrig said—died by King Orfeo's sword?"

"That is the human version of it, but we have a different story. One provided by Ankou himself."

"Ankou?"

"He is our harbinger of death, bearing witness to the end of all fae."

"Grim Reaper, fae style."

Deirdre narrowed her eyes in confusion.

"Never mind," I said. "Go on."

"Ankou tells us that the Elf King killed them all and then walked into his own death rather than draw us into war. That is the story I have been told, at least."

"Wise."

"Indeed," Deirdre said in a distant voice.

"You know that you are one of the best people I've ever met," I said, out-of-blueish. "And I've met a few. Ate a few, too."

Deirdre's eyes widened in surprise before softening with a smile.

"He's wrong, you know. Oighrig End. Wrong about you. You are not a liar, and I've never seen you play the victim. And if the other members of the UnSeelie Court are half of who you are, he's wrong about them, too."

Deirdre nodded, her gaze turning away from me in humility before she leapt (and I mean leapt) from my door's threshold to where I was lying on my bed, giving me the biggest hug.

Thankfully it was a short one, because she was literally suffocating me. "I'll bring you a plate of food," she said before skipping out of the room.

Alone, I looked at the clock. Ten to eight, which sounded about right for a girl in the prime of her life to go to bed. I turned off the lights and waited for the quiet bliss of sleep.

If I had known what waited for me on the other side of the veil, I would have done everything in my power to stay awake.

11

NIGHTMARES AND MURDERS

I've been around for a long time and had my share of bone-shattering nightmares. On more than one occasion I've woken up in a sweat, absolutely positive that what I dreamed had actually happened. Thing is, if you've done all the bad that I have, nightmares are something you get used to.

So when my dream that night turned bad, I was kind of used to it.

The thing about nightmares is, they're usually a distorted memory or some horrification of the future. Pepper in the incoherence usually associated with dreams and add a dash of heart-thumping certainty that it's really happening and presto: a full-fledged nightmare.

But the dream I was having wasn't a memory. At least, not mine. Nor did it portray some possible future. Rather, it was a vivid—what would you call it? A show, perhaps? Movie? I really don't know—experience where I was an observer, watching everything unfold through someone else's eyes.

It was like being in a video game.

If, that was, the video game involved the merciless slaughter of humans. And by humans, I don't mean pixelated representations of humans on a screen.

I mean actual, red-blooded, air-breathing, opinion-spewing

humans. I've been around enough dead bodies to know what death looks like, and this was the real deal.

And that's where this strange nightmare started: Standing over six dead bodies, four soldiers dressed in armor appropriate to the era, a squire that couldn't have been older than sixteen and a young woman who was probably in the wrong place at the wrong time.

The bodies were mangled, and from the lacerations on their faces and the way their blood stained their clothing, they didn't die well—or fast. This guy wasn't just killing them ... he was punishing them.

From the windows of his eyes, we stood on a moor with nothing in sight for miles. But then he turned around and I saw where we really were: outside an old castle, the surrounding area cleared so the guards could see enemies approaching from miles away.

A lot of good that did them. Judging by lack of shouting guards and ringing bells, it was clear that whomever lived in this castle had no idea an enemy was at their gate.

He examined the castle wall, giving me an opportunity to see it myself. From its stones and structure, I placed us somewhere in England, just after medieval times.

Without hesitation, he jumped on the wall and, using the tiny, uneven cavities and holes typical of old masonry work, he climbed the wall with the kind of speed I did not think possible for a vampire, and certainly not for a human.

Within seconds he had scaled the hundred-foot wall and climbed onto the curtain wall surrounding the castle. The two guards were taken completely by surprise, and had just enough time to let out squeals before blood-soaked hands that weren't my own grabbed them and thrust their bodies against the stone wall. I heard several cracks followed by agonized screams.

This creature—this monster—threw them against the wall hard enough that they would never walk again, but not hard enough to actually kill them. This, I sensed, was intentional. The *just shy of actually killing them* method was this monster's way of truly punishing these soldiers, because they would either get help and end up cripples the rest of their lives, or they would bleed out on the stone floor.

Either way, their next few hours would be agony. Not that the owner of these eyes cared; he simply moved on, running down the lookout tower toward the doorway leading into the castle.

Three guards with longswords came into the stone hallway, and as soon as they saw him, they charged. Stupid. His hands, empty of weapons, were out in front of him, and as the first guard swung his sword, the creature ducked before lunging forward and throwing him into the other two guards.

All three were prone on the ground. The creature grabbed the ankles of two of them and flung them over the wall, their screams following them to their deaths. The third guard tried to run, and this killing monster picked up one of the discarded longswords and threw it into the fleeing guard's back, impaling him against the wall.

The creature walked past the trapped, dying man without so much as a second glance, leaving him to groan and cry as his life slowly drained away.

Whatever this creature's mission was, he no longer cared if anyone knew he was here.

And they knew. Alarm bells rang as guards cried out, "We're under attack! We're under attack!"

I knew the drill. Now that the alarms were sounded, the guards on duty would man their posts, ready for battle, while the remaining soldiers who were sleeping or off-duty would run into the armory, where several squires would be readying their armor and weapons. In a well-trained castle, it would take a matter of minutes to arm and ready the entire garrison.

The last place any attacker would want to be was in the armory, and that's exactly where this killer went. The creature had purpose in his step—he knew the layout of the castle—and when he reached the armory, it was already half-full of soldiers preparing for war.

He walked in, and everything stopped: the clanging weapons, the shouting, the clamoring of leather straps. The room went silent as he entered, a hundred eyes on him.

Not a word was spoken until a soldier who still hadn't put on his armor grabbed a halberd and charged. The poor fool. He was dead before he took two steps.

The killer pulled in his newest victim and crushed his skull between his hands. Then he spoke in a calm voice with an accent I hadn't heard in centuries. "I will bestow upon you a gift your king failed to provide to me and my family. I shall give you a single minute. You may use that time to prepare for battle or pray to your god. I do not care. But do use your minute wisely, for it will be your last."

He walked into the center of the room and stood perfectly still. I couldn't see what most of the soldiers were doing, but from what I could hear, many took this man's advice, saying their prayers like they might on their deathbeds.

I don't know if a full minute passed or not. But when he deemed the minute to be over, he started killing. There must have been fifty men in that room, maybe more. And even with their overwhelming numbers, they didn't stand a chance.

Bones snapped and flesh tore as he made his way through them, killing one after another after another. All while they screamed.

And screamed.

And just when I thought the horror would never stop, I was awoken by screams not from the world of nightmares, but this one.

Deirdre was screaming my name. I could hear her calling me, *needing* me, and I tried to force myself awake.

I struggled to move as my consciousness swam against the currents of my nightmare before finally breaking through the veil of sleep.

I sat up in a jolt, my nightmare already fading away with unnatural speed. Not that I had time to think about that; what I had heard in my dreams was actually happening.

Deirdre was screaming.

I flung the sheets off and ran into her room where Oighrig End lay on her bed, dead.

End of Part 1

PART II
INTERMISSION

Oighrig End has sufficiently primed the needy changeling.

It's easy to bag an UnSeelie brat. Just talk about how evil their kind is, how their people were responsible for much of the evil that now exists in the mortal realm. Make them self-conscious, make them feel bad about themselves, and then swoop in with a smile and an "I understand," or "They're wrong," and presto: panties on the floor, and Oighrig End heaving atop them like a lion on a cheese grater. Go me with my Lysistrata jokes.

And this particular changeling—Deirdre, was it?—is exceptionally beautiful, he thought as he pranced around his room, preparing for tonight's festivities. A shave, a shower and some scent of lilac, the preferred fragrance of the fae. *I might even have her more than once. After all, I am stuck in this place for three days. And my only alternatives are the human and the halfling.*

The human was cute, but alas, humans lacked the vigorous pace he had grown accustomed to. Then there was the matter of the halfling. She was pretty, but she was also blind, and Oighrig End liked to look his mounts in the eyes when his, ahem ... end drew near.

He had just picked up a copy of Ovid's *Metamorphosis*—the book was a vital part of his seduction game—when his head started to spin. "Too much sipping of heavy dessert wine," he muttered to himself as he sat down on his bed. "Just a moment's rest to recharge the batteries, then downstairs to the changeling's room for further sips on her blissful teats."

"You always had a way with words," a voice said from the corner of the room.

Oighrig had thought he was alone, so when someone spoke, he leapt in fright. Literally. Onto his bed. "Who … who's there?" he said, scanning the room and seeing no one.

"An old friend."

Oighrig looked from side to side, desperate to see who it was.

"Come now. I know it has been a long, long time since we last met, but surely you haven't forgotten my voice?"

"Or mine," a second voice said.

"I … I …" Oighrig stammered.

"Why not?" the first voice said. "What is it you used to say? 'There is so much more than is known in this world, or any other.'"

"So much more," echoed a third, deeper voice.

"I often thought you should have dedicated your life to figuring out why the gods left. After all, surely one of your *revised* myths must give a clue as to that mystery."

But Oighrig End was too terrified to answer. Instead he just whimpered, "Mercy."

"But then again," the voice said, "perhaps some mysteries have no answer."

"Mercy," he repeated as the world continued to blur. He knew he was not sleepy because of the wine, but because of poison. "Mercy … please."

"Some mysteries may never be solved, but that does not mean they cannot be avenged."

"Mercy, please," Oighrig said one last time as the world spun and darkness enveloped him.

"Mercy?" the voice said. "I'm afraid that died in me centuries ago."

12

ACCUSATIONS, MUCH?

eirdre's screams didn't just draw me in. Within moments, Orange and Remi had appeared, both in nightgowns. The rest had yet to make their way to the room (with the exception of the abatwas—Snap, Crackle and Pop—who, for all I knew, stood in the room somewhere, camouflaged by the old Persian carpet and their tiny size).

"What happened, Deirdre?" I asked, trying to get her attention.

She didn't look at me, her gaze fixed on Oighrig End. "I ... I ... don't know. He asked if I was interested in a nightcap. I told him my hair did not need such sleep aids, and he laughed, saying he meant a drink so that we could continue our conversation. I agreed, and he said he would come to my room in an hour. I decided to use that time to shower and prepare my questions for our continued conversation. When I emerged from the bathroom, I saw him here. Dead."

"A likely story," Orange said, "changeling." He spat that last word as if it were sour milk.

"Hold on a second," I said, stepping between Orange and Deirdre. "She would never—"

"Never what?" Remi said. "Kill, maim, destroy? I don't know how well-versed you are in the ways of the UnSeelie Court, but of all the gods' creations, few are as vicious as changelings."

"That's nice, coming from a human soldier." I turned on my heels to take that sanctimonious human head on. "I'm fairly sure if we took an honest look at capacities for destruction, your kind would take the proverbial, blood-soaked cake."

" 'Your kind'?" Remi said, lifting an eyebrow.

"Soldiers, warriors … Canadian Armed Forces," I growled. "Besides, how do we know it wasn't you? You were quite aggressive in your questioning."

"How dare you? Remi LaChance is one of the gentlest—"

"Thank you, Orange, but please. This is one fight I'm determined to have on my own," Remi said, extending a placating hand to Orange. Then, looking down at me, he clenched his gloved hands. "Young lady, do not confuse curiosity with aggression. I would no more hurt Oighrig End than—"

"Pick up a gun? Fight in a war? Given that you are, by your own proclamation, a seasoned soldier, I find it hard to accept the 'conscientious objector' defense. Besides, why are you wearing gloves? Didn't want to leave behind fingerprints?"

"I had the same thought, milady," Deirdre said. "Gloved hands hide guilty fingers."

Remi lifted his gloved hands in a very self-conscious manner before regaining his scowl. "I have a condition, and am very self-conscious about my hands. My gloves are not an indication of guilt, but merely a sign of my shyness and further proof of my sensitive nature. And one more thing, my dear young lady. Where were you when—"

"What … what is going on?" a soft voice asked.

Although the voice was low, we all stopped arguing and turned. Sarah stood with her black guide dog at the bedroom door's threshold. Her head was tilted so her left ear faced us, and she wore a confused, almost frightened look. Behind her stood Jarvis and Freol, both staring at Oighrig End's body with silent, disbelieving eyes.

"It seems, my dear, that our guest of honor has met an untimely end," Remi said in a cautious tone.

"By the hands of our changeling guest," Orange added.

"I did no such thing." Deirdre's voice quavered as if trying to hold back tears.

"You arrogant Seelie Court, biased moron," I turned to Orange. "We don't go throwing around accusations based on racial profiling."

"Why not?" Orange asked. I could tell the question was genuine; he really didn't understand my objections, and from the way he waited for my response, I gathered that the Seelie Court *did* judge on the basis of where people came from, their particular subspecies, and all sorts of other racially motivated profiling.

"Because," I said as an oh so witty comeback.

Remi sighed, and I thought he was going to renew his attack on Deirdre, but instead he said, "The young lady is right: we cannot assume that just because one has the capacity to kill, they have actually killed. We have, as of yet, no proof that the changeling is the murderer. That is not how things are done anymore. Not since the gods left, at least."

Orange gave Remi a look that could have shattered glass, and Remi, by way of self-defense, shrugged.

"I do apologize," Sarah said, "but I am at a visual disadvantage. Oighrig End is dead?"

I nodded, and then realized how ridiculous nodding was. "Yes."

"How?" Sarah asked.

The question drove home, because in my desperation to defend Deirdre, I had never examined the body. I walked over to Oighrig End and, without touching him, took a closer look at his wounds.

"Oh please," Orange said in a condescending tone, "what could you possibly be looking for? He was stabbed."

"Yes," I said, still examining the body. Deirdre and Remi did the same. "But there is much we can learn from a stab wound."

Remi gave me a curious look.

"Forensics class. I'm thinking of training as a policeman. Well, woman."

"I see." Remi returned his gaze to the body.

The three of us took a closer look. Whoever killed Oighrig End did so in a fit of abject hate; he had been stabbed multiple times all over his chest, but the wounds had no pattern.

Usually when someone stabs their victim multiple times, they do so at a particular angle, and the radius of the wounds are closely bunched together, all penetrating the body from that angle. But Oighrig End's wounds were all over his chest, and the angles made no sense, as if the killer had switched hands in the middle of the stabbing.

And there was one more unusual thing: the wounds varied in intensity. Some were light, barely scratches. Others were deep cuts, obviously inflicted by powerful hands.

Whoever killed Oighrig End must have done so in a fit of rage and doubt to inflict such a wide array of wounds. And from my best guess, that meant the killer both loved and hated the man. This was a tidbit I'd keep to myself, given how much Deirdre revered Oighrig End and how deeply she was hurt by his insults.

I looked up to see that Remi had concluded his investigation quite quickly, evidently ascertaining everything he could with a cursory glance. Either he didn't know enough about these types of wounds to really learn anything (which meant he was a lot less experienced than he claimed), or he had seen something that satisfied his curiosity.

Deirdre circled the body before leaning in close. Then she did that thing she always does when surprised or wanting to keep a secret: her eyes widened slightly and her nose flared. That girl should never play poker.

I quickly looked at Remi to see if he had noticed, but he was too busy lost in thought, presumably mulling over everything *his* investigation of the body revealed to him. *Good,* I thought, filing this away to ask her about later.

Whatever Deirdre saw was enough for her, and she backed away from the body toward the wall, where she stood erect and still, saying nothing. The changeling guard stance. It looked impassive, but given the way changelings were trained in combat, that stance meant she was ready to pounce at a moment's notice.

I knew that. So did the others.

Way to not admit guilt, Deirdre, I thought, and backed away from the body myself. "OK, I'm done."

"And are you satisfied?" Orange asked.

"Not really. I still have no idea who did this. But at least I know more than I did before."

"And what have you learned?" Sarah asked.

"No—not now, and not here. Besides, I want to know what Soldier Boy here knows, too. I suggest we head to the conference room where we can hurl accusations at one another while we wait for the authorities to show up."

Orange shifted nervously at the mention of the police.

"What?" I asked the ugly elf. "Nervous to have real detectives searching for clues?"

"No, not at all," he said with an uneven, nervous grin. "It's just the storm. It's killed all communications and, well—until the storm passes, I'm afraid we're on our own."

13
YOU DID IT! NO, YOU DID!

*S*o *we're on our own,* I thought as I looked out the window of the lecture hall. Outside, heavy snow fell in a near curtain of white.

My cell phone's screen read Call Failed with the name Egya above it. I couldn't reach him—or anyone, for that matter. Even the internet didn't work, nor did any of the landlines in the Douglas Hall offices. Orange wasn't kidding when he said we were cut off.

I turned to see everyone milling about in the room. Well, everyone except Oighrig End. He was still lying on Deirdre's bed. Sarah sat on the stage holding her dog close, petting his gruff, black-furred neck. Jack was at the back, standing perfectly still. Remi paced the back of the room, the abatwas huddled together on the speakers and Deirdre stood at the back of room in her aggressive changeling stance. As for the rest, Jarvis, Freol and Orange sat on the outermost seats, as if they wanted to be as far apart as possible.

There was something off about all of them, but especially Freol. It bugged me that he didn't speak and didn't seem to acknowledge me or anyone else. He just stared impassively at a space on the wall, still dressed in that funeral suit.

Every now and then, one of them would look out at the falling snow with a heavy sigh. That no one could get to us was one thing. Now we were not only on our own, but our cellphones didn't work, the internet was down … we were literally cut off from the world. When I was a young vampire, it was normal to find yourself somewhere far from others, alone and with no way to talk to anyone.

But in the modern world, the constant ability to reach someone—anyone—became a part of who we are. We're so used to being connected that when those tethers to the outside world are cut, we get nervous. These fae may have only been introduced to cell phones and the World Wide Web a few years ago, but they were used to these modern comforts and were just as nervous as any human would be about being cut off.

Add to that a dead body lying on a double bed upstairs and, well, it made sense that everyone was shaken up. I suspected every time they looked out the window, they were trying to will the snow away.

↔

No one spoke, no one looked at each other, and we might have stayed that way for a long time had I not thought out loud, *Anyone here is strong enough to have killed him.*

"Including you," Orange said.

"Orange," Sarah said in an admonishing tone, "you're not helping."

"Maybe," the ugly elf admitted, "but I'm also not going to let Miss Human over there play innocent."

"You know," Remi said, stopping his pacing, "I am curious about you, Miss Darling. You claim to be a schoolgirl, but what Sarah and Orange told me is that you pulled out a checkbook from a very expensive purse and paid for three tickets like it was nothing."

"I'm rich," I said. "I won't apologize for that."

"Nor should you have to. We're all rich here. Me: inheritance," he gestured that it was my turn to tell them where my money came from.

71

I put a hand on my chest and said in an exaggerated tone, "Me: none of your business."

"Fair enough," Remi said. "But I have encountered many rich young ladies in my time, and none of them would so happily and fearlessly examine a dead body like you did."

"Like I said, I'm thinking of going into law enforcement," I lied.

"Please," Remi said, "don't bullshit a bullshitter."

"And what exactly are you bullshitting about?"

"Oh shut it, the both of you," Orange screamed. "I've had enough of this. Law enforcement might not be able to make it to us, but we can make it to them. I'm leaving."

"You can't," I said.

"Why not?"

"Because everyone needs to stay here until they arrive. We're all suspects until someone with authority comes to sort us out. We don't want one of us escaping when—"

"Are you accusing me of being the killer?" Orange asked.

"If the wig fits."

"Why you insolent, sniveling little ..."

I took a step toward him, fists clenched.

Deirdre saw my aggressive stance and took a step forward herself.

Big mistake, because as soon as the changeling showed her anger, Jack the giant stood up and took two massive steps toward her.

From the way Deirdre moved, I was pretty sure she'd fought giants before. She tucked in real low and waited for Jack to swing. As soon as his arm was in mid-motion, she tumbled forward and to the left and gave the back of his knee a bone-crushing kick.

He went down to one knee and with his other hand grabbed Deirdre's legs. Evidently this giant had experience fighting changelings.

Deirdre clawed at Jack's hands, drawing blood as her powerful nails dug into his skin.

They might have literally torn each other apart if Remi and I hadn't rushed over to them. "Deirdre, enough!" I yelled, placing my hands on her.

"Jack," Remi said, "please stop this. Now." Remi's voice sounded like a battlefield command, and Jack immediately let go. So much for Remi bullshitting about seeing action. Only someone who had led troops in battle could have given such an unignorable command.

As soon as the word "Now" left his lips, Jack let go.

Pulling—as much as you can pull someone stronger than a rhino—at our respective fae, Remi and I managed to get the two warriors to opposite ends of the room.

"Enough, Deirdre," I said.

The changeling was breathing hard, her fingers covered in green blood. That was the thing about Others: they didn't bleed red like humans. Valkyrie bled yellow, dwarves a dust-colored brown, angels bled light and fae bled various shades of green depending on their type and powers.

Seeing her blood-stained hands, I had a thought. When I had examined the body, I only saw red. But whoever killed Oighrig End did so in an extremely violent manner. There was no way you could inflict so much damage on the man without hurting yourself. And that doesn't include anything he would have done to try to escape.

Murder victims don't just lie there. They scratch, punch, bite, throw things. The murder scene should have had a bit of non-red blood around, but it didn't.

That meant one of two things: either Oighrig End wasn't killed in Deirdre's room, or the killer was human.

↔

Of course, that's what I thought. Convincing seven people I was right was another thing.

"All I'm saying is that there would be a couple drops of green blood somewhere."

"But there weren't," Remi said.

"Exactly," I said. "So that means either you or I are the killers, given that we bleed red, or he was killed somewhere else."

"Are you serious?" Orange yelped. "I don't see how you can make such assumptions with what we know."

"You're right," I agreed, looking at the others, "but we should at least look in everyone's rooms and—"

"Look for what?"

"Clues."

"Clues?"

"Yes, because the more I think about it, the more I'm convinced one of you bastards is trying to frame the poor, innocent UnSeelie Court girl."

"Because there was no green blood," Sarah said, not so much asking a question, but digesting the clues.

"Exactly," I said. "I'm starting to think it was Mrs. Peacock in the library with the candlestick."

"Who the hell is Mrs. Peacock?" Orange growled.

"No one," I said. "Just a human joke." I looked at Remi for backup, but evidently he didn't find me humorous at all.

"OK, so we shall walk into each other's room and look for clues," Sarah said.

"That's what I propose," I said.

"Very well," Sarah said, standing up. "Where shall we start?"

"Jack's room is on this floor. As good a place as any." I looked over at the giant, who grunted the same way a walrus might warn us to get out of his territory.

14

SPOTLESS ROOMS AND DIRTY KITCHENS

*W*e started with the downstairs, me leading the morbid procession. Our first stop: the giant's room. It was very neat, considering how small the room was compared to his grand stature. The only thing of note was that his mattress was on the floor, presumably because he was too big to sleep on a bed frame.

I looked around the room and, other than the mattress, saw that Jack had a bottle of Oban whisky in his room. No green or red blood, no sign of a struggle, no murder weapon.

Next.

We went from room to room, and outside of finding nothing, the only surprising thing was how neat everyone was: made beds, folded clothes, toothbrushes in toiletry bags, toothpaste caps on. These fae, unlike my UnSeelie Court changeling of a roommate, were immaculately tidy. And as for the one human, he even had the next day's clothes laid out on his bed. Uber tidy, but then he did have a butler, so …

"This is going nowhere," I said after we walked out of Sarah's room, the last one in our macabre game of *Clue*.

"See," Orange said, "I told you."

"You did," I said, nodding in agreement.

I guess the ugly elf had prepared for a retort, and me agreeing surprised him. "Ahh, thank you?" he said, more as a question than a statement.

"But just because we didn't find anything doesn't mean the killer isn't one of us. All it means is the killer is smart. Which, in this case, means dangerous."

"Indeed," Remi said. "Tell me, young lady … as one who wishes to go into law enforcement, what do you suggest we do now?"

"Well, I guess a detective would interrogate the suspects."

"I agree," Remi said, "but given that we all are suspects, how does a detective interrogate him *or herself*?"

"She *or he* doesn't," I said, "but if we have several detectives, then that's another story."

↔

We all gathered once more in the lecture hall, where a simple plan was outlined: we would all question one another and write down our answers. Then we would read out our notes so that everyone got each other's answers. Think of it as speed dating, only substitute finding a murderer instead of a date.

Using an egg timer to keep each interview under ten minutes, we lined up several chairs into two rows, and then, armed with note-books and pens, we started one of the most awkward multi-level cross-examinations of all time.

↔

The first person I interviewed was Sarah. I started with the obvious question: "Where were you after dinner?"

Her dog let a huff, as if that was a stupid question.

Sarah, on the other hand, was kinder. "My room. I was quite exhausted with the day's preparations and, well, as exciting as it was to be in Professor End's presence, I was glad to crawl into my bed."

"Is this your first time in Douglas Hall?"

She tilted her head, giving me more ear than face. "Yes, other than the two visits when we were deciding on the lecture venue."

"Given that you haven't spent much time here, how did you get from the dining hall to your room?"

Again her dog Tiny snorted. This time Sarah put a hand on his head as if to say *Relax*. "Tiny guided me."

"That's quite impressive for a dog," I said, giving the canine a dirty look, "no matter how smart or well-trained."

"Oh, yes," she said with an embarrassed smile, "Remi LaChance was kind enough to escort us to our room."

"Escort ... and leave?" I asked.

"Of course. What are you trying to say?" Sarah set a hand on her chest. Her dog let out a little growl just to punctuate her indignation.

"Just that Remi is an attractive man, and—"

"He may be attractive, but I fear that doesn't really factor into my considerations when choosing whom to bed with." She looked at me head-on as she spoke, removing her sunglasses and widening her eyes so I could get a good look at them.

Most irises, even those belonging to blind people, were a cloudlike kaleidoscope of green or blue or brown around a black pupil. Sarah's eyes weren't that at all: her irises were less cloudlike and more fractal, as if they had been made of a crystal that exploded from the pupil out. Each shard was the standard green and blue common to eyes, but they possessed a light halo of red.

"They're ... they're amazing," I stammered.

"So I've been told," she said. "When I first went blind, all I heard was how unique they looked, how beautiful I was because of these dead things in my skull."

"You weren't born blind?"

She shook her head. "I lost my sight in an accident when I was eight, and all the magic in the Seelie Court could do nothing to make them work again."

"I'm sorry," I said. "Can I ask what happened?"

"You can ask," Sarah said, "but only my friends know what happened, and we are not friends. Not yet, and given your demeanor, I doubt ever." Those words, as harsh as they were, weren't said to hurt my feelings or insult me—they were just matter-of-fact.

"True, and I apologize for overstepping my boundaries. What happened to you when you were eight has little bearing on what's happening now," I said. "Just one last question: Did you know anyone here before the event? Either after the gods left, or during your time in the Seelie Court."

"Humph," she said. "That's like asking an Australian if they know a George from Melbourne. The Seelie Court is—well, *was* a vast domain."

"I know, but indulge me. Have you ever met anyone here prior to this event?"

"Other than Orange from my work at FSA, no." And as if the little timer heard her "no," there was a ding, indicating it was time to interview the next person.

15

EGG-TIMERS AND ALIBIS

*T*he next few interviews were a montage of useless information.

ME: So Orange, where were you at the time of the murder?

ORANGE: Cleaning up the kitchen after dinner.

ME: Strange. Isn't that the abatwas' role?

ORANGE: And pay them overtime? Do you have any idea what Oighrig End's speaker fee was? Let alone renting this hall? I cut costs wherever I could.

DING!

ME: So Snap, Crackle and Pop, after the dinner, where were you?

ABATWAS: Answer in such a furry of high-squeaked noises that I can't understand a word.

ME: OK, let's try that again. Thumbs up for YES, do nothing for NO. After dinner, were the three of you together?

ABATWAS: Three thumbs up.

ME: Good. Were you cleaning up?

ABATWAS: One thumb up, two nothings.

ME: OK. Crackle, why were you cleaning up when your two friends here were doing nothing?

CRACKLE: Gestures that the other two were sleeping.

ME: Orange said he cleaned up because he didn't want to pay you guys overtime.

ABATWAS: Thumbs up, and then the three of them rub their thumbs and forefingers together—the universal gesture for penny-pinching.

DING!

ME: Remi, did you see anything?

REMI: Nope. I retired as soon as after-dinner drinks were done.

ME: Went to bed?

REMI: Straight to it.

ME: Anything else I should know?

REMI: Nothing comes to mind.

DING!

ME: Jarvis, did you join them for dinner?

JARVIS: Sadly, no. I prepared Mr. LaChance's clothes for the next day and retired at around 7pm.

DING!

ME: Freol Garfum, where were you after the dinner party ended?

FREOL: (Silence)

ME: Mr. Garfum?

FREOL: (More silence)

ME: You don't speak, do you?

FREOL: (Even more silence)

DING!

. . .

My last interview was with Jack the giant, and I swore that even if he admitted to killing the professor, I'd proclaim him innocent just for saying something other than that he was in bed.

"And what about you, Jack? Where were you? And please don't say you were in bed," I started to ask the giant, but stopped when I saw what hung around his neck.

With him seated, I could actually see the giant up close. While I had noticed something around his neck before, I hadn't seen what it was. Now I saw it: a single silver chain as thick as a thread of silk. At its end were two heavy, intertwined silver rings.

The size and obvious weight of the rings should have been enough to snap the thread on which they hung, but I knew the thread would never break under the weight of the rings.

They would never break under the weight of anything in this world or any other.

But that wasn't something I could deal with now. Now I needed to finish my questioning. "Jack," I repeated, "where were you?"

Jack let out a sigh so heavy it literally blew my hair back, and gestured that he had been sleeping.

"Can anyone corroborate that?"

He shook his head, but his eyes lit with a thought. He gestured for me to follow, and took me to the stairwell leading to Deirdre's room. There he took two steps up, showing me how he literally was too large to climb up.

Talk about an O.J., gloves-don't-fit-the-hand alibi.

16

WIND-DOWNS AND WHAT'S NEXT

*M*y interviews were straightforward enough. When it came time for me to be questioned, most of what people wanted to ask me had already been asked and answered.

Why did I attend?

"To support my friend."

How was I able to purchase the tickets?

"I'm rich. And no, it's none of your business how I got my money."

Had I ever heard of Professor Oighrig End before?

"Is the fact that I practically fell asleep during his lecture answer enough?"

Perhaps the most original question came from Orange, who asked me in that vile tone of his, "How do you like being friends with a changeling?"

My answer was to flip his orange wig off his head. The bald skull beneath was a crimson, blood red. He quickly picked up his mangled wig and put it on his head. "If—if you weren't a girl and a human, I'd kick you out of the building and into the snow, you … you …"

"That's enough," Sarah said, and guided by Tiny, she walked over to Orange and helped put his wig on, which given the professional relationship they had, she did with surprising dexterity. "Ms. Darling, I think you owe Orange an apology."

"OK," I said, watching the orange rag wiggle back and forth on his head while he adjusted it, "I apologize."

"Thank you," Sarah said, taking Orange's hand to guide him away from me.

"Sorry, one last question …"

"Your interview is over," Orange said, spittle spewing out his lips.

"I don't think so," I said. "Hate me as much as you like. We're still looking for a murderer, and your answers could provide vital clues."

"I will never—"

"Please, Orange," Sarah said, "cooperate." Orange's face twisted in defiant rage, but before he could say another word, Sarah added, "For all of us. Please."

Orange looked around the room and sighed. "For group cohesion, fine. One last question."

"Your skull … it's red. Why?"

That sent Orange into a rage. "Are you mocking me? Me?" he screamed, breaking away from Sarah's grasp and running toward me.

He didn't get two steps in before Deirdre stood between us. I thought she was going to attack him again, but this time the changeling took a more diplomatic stance. "Please answer milady."

"It is not relevant to the investigation," he cried out.

"Is it not?" Deirdre said. "Surely you have heard of the goblin Redcap?" As the name escaped Deirdre's lips, I cried out a quiet— almost entirely in my head—"Hurray!"

Everyone looked at me.

OK, not as quiet as I wanted, but still, good for Deirdre. She was thinking exactly what I was: Redcap, the grand, murderous goblin who resided on the borders between the UnSeelie Court and the mortal plane. It's legend that the goblin's bald scalp would magically turn into the color of his latest victim's blood.

"You wouldn't dare imply that I am one as horrid as Redcap the Horrible?"

"I am not implying that you could be as horrid as Redcap. He was a vile and corrupt being," she said.

Orange nodded in satisfaction.

"But what I am saying," Deirdre said in a voice loud enough for everyone to hear, "is that you may be a sniveling little Seelie Court— what is the mortal term for it?—ahh yes, fanboy to Redcap. A cheap imitation who, like his hero, also paints his bald head with the blood of his victims."

I expected Deirdre's insult to send Orange over the edge, perhaps far enough that the outclassed elf might even try to strike the changeling. But instead, he pursed his lips almost as if he expected Deirdre to insult him in such a way.

With a venomous tone, he pulled out a vial from his pocket and said, "Raspberry and elderflower essence mixed with brown sugar. It makes for a far more effective wig glue than anything mortals can concoct." He opened the vial, dipped in his finger and licked it. Then he poured a little out for Deirdre to taste.

The changeling sniffed it. "Your words smell true."

"Indeed," the ugly elf said. He stuck a finger between his wig line and scalp and vigorously rubbed his head. Pulling out a finger covered in red, he said, "Seems elf sweat causes mortal glues to lose their stickiness. But my recipe is only strengthened by my body's fluids. Care to taste?"

He held his finger out to Deirdre, who took a step back.

"Didn't think so." He pulled out a handkerchief and wiped his hands clean.

Satisfied that he had put Deirdre and me in our places, the ugly elf looked at his watch. "It is nearly five o'clock. We can compare our notes after our stomachs are filled. Might I suggest we have an early dinner and, if the mood strikes us, another round of accusations, finger-pointing and passive-aggressive comments? Or perhaps an early night? Who knows, maybe the GoneGods will smile upon us this evening and clear the snow enough for the authorities to arrive so we can leave this infernal place. Agreed?"

"Shouldn't we share our notes first?" I asked in that passive-aggressive way I am oh so good at.

Orange looked at me, then my stomach. GoneGod damn it, the ugly elf was right: I was hungry. We all were. I shrugged, then nodded.

"Then it's settled?" Orange said.

His question was met with silence—which, given the somber mood we were all in, was taken as consent. Had I known what kind of dessert was in store for us, I would have protested with every fiber of my now soulless human body.

17
POLITE DINNER DISCUSSIONS AND IMPOLITE DESSERT DISASTERS

*B*ecause of the inconvenient murder, there was no dinner planned for us. No cooked goose, no cranberry sauce, mashed peas, potatoes, parsnips or carrots. There were just a bunch of raw ingredients. So much for Christmas Eve dinner.

The goose would remain in the fridge, but the rest of the stuff could be cooked. Turning on ovens and stovetops, we boiled the carrots and peas, baked the potatoes and grilled the parsnips.

Not bad. And given that I was a vegetarian, things could have been worse.

We didn't even bother to go to the dining hall. All of us ate our garden-variety vegetarian treats standing silent in the kitchen. Deirdre and I leaned against an oven door, Sarah offered pieces of her meal to Tiny the dog, and the abatwas' plates floated a few inches off the ground.

The only noises came from our forks against our plates—except for Jack the giant, who'd set aside the tiny utensil—and the smacking of our lips. It was the most depressing Christmas Eve ever, and given I was already feeling like crap, this just sank me further into my black hole of despair.

I hate this. I looked up to see if anyone had reacted and realized I had said that in my head when I had meant to say it out loud. "I hate this."

My voice echoed in the kitchen and all eyes were on me. "I hate this," I repeated. "It's Christmas Eve, and we didn't even bother to pull out cloth napkins. Look, I know someone died and all, but if I don't get at least a hint of Christmas cheer, I'm going to ..." I realized I had talked myself into a corner. I couldn't say "kill someone" or "off myself." It would have been a joke, but this crowd was a wee bit sensitive to stuff like that.

"Spontaneously combust," Sarah offered.

Some polite giggles.

"Yes," I said, snapping my fingers. "And spontaneous combustion is messy. Trust me, I've done it before."

"What do you suggest?" Remi said.

"I don't know. A song, maybe? Don't elves and fairies love to sing?"

"Very well, young lady. Allow me." Remi moved to the center of the kitchen and cleared his throat before singing a very off-tune, nearly offensive "Jingle Bells."

He belted out two lines before people started playfully booing him into silence. "Not to your liking?" he said with a grin. "Then perhaps someone else would like to take the mike? Orange?"

"There isn't a wig in the world that could beautify my singing," the ugly elf said with a chuckle.

"Deirdre? Katrina?"

We both shook our heads.

"Well, the giant doesn't speak, and I doubt Freol will surprise us by suddenly speaking. As for Jarvis, as strong as the poor trow is, he cannot carry a tune. The abatwas' screeching is sure to drive us mad, so that leaves only you, dear Sarah. Legend says halflings are gifted with the power of song. Is this true?"

"Perhaps," Sarah said, a coy smile tiptoeing onto her face.

"Then please," Remi said, "save us from ourselves with your song."

"Because you ask this of me, then I shall," she said in that matter-of-fact tone she had used on me earlier. "But I fear I don't know many songs of cheer."

"Then regale us with something that will stir our souls. Anything is better than what we are feeling now."

"Very well," Sarah said, stepping forward. And she started singing a song in Elvish that was unlike anything I have ever heard before.

↔

Of all the Others that landed on Earth, perhaps the most complicated ones are fae. Broadly speaking—and I am generalizing, stereotyping and type-casting—fae fall into two camps: The Seelie and UnSeelie Courts, Light and Dark, except to simplify them as such is a mistake. In the world of fae, the Light isn't always good, and the Dark isn't always evil. Their mortality spectrum has a thousand shades of gray (I'm sure there's a *Fifty Shades of Grey* joke here somewhere, but can we say *overdone*, people?), and the divide between the two courts tends to be along the lines of beauty. Seelie Court members are pretty: elves, pixies, fairies. UnSeelie Court not so much: trolls, goblins, trows.

Not that UnSeelie don't have their share of beauty. Take Deirdre as case and point: she's gorgeous. But she's also a trained killer whose methods tend to be kidnapping and torture. Pretty ugly stuff.

But the divide between pretty and ugly isn't the only thing that makes fae strange. They all seem to have some sort of condition to their being. Kelpie can grant wishes and they don't have to burn time to do it, either. Leprechauns *do* have pots of gold. Dwellings *do* magically appear under any bridge if a troll is nearby.

It seems that their nature is magic, and that magic varies from fae to fae. Think of it like this: every fae has a thing, and a halfling's thing is song.

They can sing.

And the thing about a halfling's song is that it's not about the music, or even the words. Halfling music is about emotion. It touches our very being, forcing out emotions that are powerful, real and undeniable.

To hear a halfling sing is to unlock feelings you didn't know you had. Sarah sang like one possessed by the divine.

Her song started out lovely enough, evoking pleasant feelings that soon turned into emotions I associate with love. But it was more than love, for as much as I think I've known what it feels like to be in love, what I felt listening to her was so much more.

It wasn't just the feeling of love. It was love itself, and soon that love turned into love coupled with joy.

Given how horrible I'd been feeling these last few weeks, it was incredible to have those emotions—emotions I couldn't seem to find in myself anymore—brought back to me with such intensity.

I didn't want this to ever stop, and when both love and joy became sadness, I found myself wiping away violent and sudden tears. Looking around me, I saw everyone was affected the same way I was. Even Sarah, whose eyes were like exploding universes, released tears down her freckled cheeks.

Soon the sadness was replaced with acceptance and joy again, only for great anger to follow it.

The anger I felt at that moment in her song was greater than any rage I had ever felt before, total and complete. I knew if the undefined source of that anger were presented to me, I would kill it without a moment's hesitation.

Mercifully, the anger stopped. Not subsided, or dissolved or became less intense, but stopped as if the bearer of that anger had been destroyed. A void filled my heart—a void that slowly filled with obsession and determination.

It felt as if renewed purpose had entered her song, before both anger and relief mingled inside me. Then the anger subsided, slowly this time, and all that was left was relief that slowly became joy again.

And with that, Sarah's song had ended.

Wiping away tears, I saw that everyone was crying. And when

Remi had dabbed away his own tears, he walked over to Sarah and offered her his handkerchief.

The halfling bard took it, wiping away her own tears as Remi said with love and admiration, "I'm glad to know your eyes are good for something."

Sarah laughed and wiped away more tears still. "If only to show my human half."

↔

Sarah's song, as emotionally devastating as it was, did serve to get us out of our funk. So much so that, when Jarvis suggested ice cream, we cheered. Well, most of us did. Freol and Jack kept their ever-silent vigil.

Strawberry, vanilla and chocolate were distributed in bowls, and we all started munching away, our moods lifted.

Jack was standing alone by the freezer, and I walked over. There was something I wanted to ask him without anyone overhearing. I climbed onto the metal counter next to him so that I was just very short beside him as opposed to nearly invisible. "Gleipnir chain?"

His eyes widened in surprise, questioning how I knew.

"I dated an elf. But that's a ..."—I put a finger over my lips—"shush."

"Shuush." Jack imitated my gesture with a smile and a wink.

"My ex-boyfriend—the elf—he told me all about Gleipnir chains. Forged by dwarves because the Norse gods needed a leash strong enough to hold Fenrir the Great Wolf. They made it from six impossible materials: the spittle of a bird, the sinew of a bear, the beard of a woman, the sound of a cat's footfall, the roots of a mountain and ... and ..." I couldn't remember the last one.

Jack made the gesture of a fish swimming, and then cupping his mouth, let out a heavy breath.

"Yeah, of course—the breath of a fish. My elf boyfriend also told me that the fae only wear one of these in atonement for a great failure." I reached out to touch the silver rings, looking at the giant to see if it was all right to touch them.

Jack nodded, and placing my hand against the rings, I could feel their heavy nature. "These rings symbolize the burden the wearer feels, and are imbued with the force of gravity itself," I said. "They are of the exact weight their wearer can manage. And as the wearer's strength increases, so too does the weight of the rings."

Jack nodded.

"There's one more thing about these rings," I said. "The wearer chooses to bear them. In other words, no one forced you to put these on. Whatever you did—"

Jack shook his head.

"Then failed to do?"

The giant nodded.

"OK then—whatever you failed to do must weigh heavily on your heart?"

The giant with the Gleipnir chain winced as if the memory of what had happened slapped him.

"I see. Is that why you do not speak? Is that part of your penance?"

Again the giant nodded.

"I understand burdens well," I said, pulling back my sleeve and revealing a tattoo of two rings that looked like his. "I got these after the gods left. A reminder of the penance I must pay for something I did."

Jack gave me a knowing look.

"I know the interviews are over, but I wanted to ask you something off the record, something I'm not obligated to write down in our shared notes. Which brings me to my question: Oighrig End's death. Does that have anything to do with these?" I touched the links again.

The giant shook his head, but I swear I saw his eyes flicker almost imperceptibly at my question.

I was considering pushing it further when Snap scampered up the giant's clothing with the kind of speed that would have made the Flash green with envy.

He whispered something in Jack's ear and, as he spoke, the giant became visibly angry. Jack cracked his knuckles, and the sound that came from his hands was thunder.

18

CHASES AND MIRAGES

*J*ack stomped out of the kitchen and toward the walk-in pantry down the hall. Rather than walking, I jumped on the giant's back and went for the ride.

The giant was too large to enter, but I wasn't. Jumping off him, I walked into what looked like a perfectly normal pantry. There was nothing unusual about it.

Crackle was on the third shelf where mostly beans and canned corn were stored. He frantically pointed at a stack of tuna cans, his high-pitched screeching at a near frenzy. I looked at the side of the can and saw green blood.

There was a ring of green from where the abatwas had moved the cans. Next to it was Pop, holding his leg. Crackle had used some thread that might have once served as his belt to make a tourniquet for Pop's severed leg.

Someone had dropped a can of tuna on his leg, severing it from his body. Pop had mercifully passed out.

The others were gathering, but Jack wouldn't let any of them into the pantry.

"Who did this?" I asked. That's when Snap jumped onto a safety map hanging on the pantry wall. He slammed his hand onto the back storage room behind the kitchen.

Without a word, Jack and I ran to the back.

"Where are you going, milady?"

"Out, Deirdre. You stay here and make sure no one leaves the room."

↔

The area wasn't very big, and given how snowed in we were, there wasn't really anywhere for—who? The killer? The abatwa maimer? Whoever—to go. We hustled down into Douglas Hall's basement, which was really just a long hallway running along the sections of the large mansion. Several doors sat on either side of the hall, but unlike Gardner Hall, they weren't accommodations but a variety of rooms, from the boiler to storage rooms.

Since there was no easy way out, we had the luxury of going down the hall, investigating each room one by one as we tightened the net.

But there was a problem: Jack was so big he hardly fit into the hallway. He hunched over so his massive shoulders scraped against the ceiling. And with every step he took, he clogged the hallway so no one could run past us. It also meant that no one could come in from behind us, either. If someone from the group wanted to head us off, they'd have to enter the basement from the upper levels.

Since Jack was too big for the hallway, he was *way* too big for the rooms. That meant I'd have to go in alone, and if there was trouble, I'd face it on my own. Sure, I could always tell the killer that he (or she) would be up against a giant when they eventually had to leave the room, but that wouldn't necessarily stop the killer from taking me out while one of the strongest beings in existence stood outside, powerless to help me.

Sometimes being small sucks, I thought as I walked into the first room. It was an unlocked pantry with two freezers, shelves of canned goods and no killer.

The next two doors were storage and, after breaking the lock (something I was sure would be taken out of the FSA's venue deposit), both rooms were empty. The next one was the boiler room, also empty.

We continued down the hall until we came across the middle room door with a padlock on the outside. "Probably not in there," I said, jostling the padlock.

Jack shook his head and made a gesture that reminded me of Harry Potter using his wand to cast a spell. Harry Potter, or Mickey Mouse in *Fantasia*. Take your pick.

"True," I said, sighing. "He could have gone in and locked it from the outside using magic."

Jack nodded, pleased with my *Charades* skills, and crushed the metal lock between his finger and thumb like one might pop bubble wrap. With the door open, he made an *after you* gesture.

"Great, let the lady walk into the dark room alone with no backup. I've never seen this scene play out before."

Except usually I'm the one hiding in the dark, I thought—quietly.

I walked into the room that was filled with pipes and large vents. So this was where everything came into the building: electricity, gas, water. Everything but sewage, though I was confident I would find a manhole somewhere, too.

Because Montreal was one of the coldest cities in the world, with an annual snowfall rivaling Siberia, water and other things that flowed through pipes and into our homes needed to be below the frost line. Six feet (I wonder if that's where six feet under comes from. Don't want to freeze and preserve the dead forever).

Also, since we were on a mountain—well, technically an inactive volcano—buildings on the slope tended to be even deeper. And this utility room did not disappoint, its slope pushing further into the ground.

As big as this room was, there was only so far one could go into the place before you met actual walls that only the pipes and vents could get through.

I scanned the room, looking for any indication that someone was here. I saw nothing, and looking at the undisturbed dust on the ground, knew that no one was here.

Another dead end, I thought, turning to leave.

That's when I heard it: an almost imperceptible breath, probably the killer letting out a sigh of relief as I turned. So he must have used magic to not only lock the door from the outside, but also cover his tracks.

Since the room was dark—and as pretty as my eyes were, I couldn't see in the dark (not anymore, at least)—I had one chance to see him. Gauging where the sigh came from, I fished out my phone from my pocket and thumbed on my flashlight. (And yay me for doing that one-handed and without looking. Then again, the fact that I could do that meant I spent way too much time on my phone, so bad me. Bad.)

I turned, pulling out my phone and flashing it over whatever was inside. And what I saw was a blood-covered dark elf who growled at me. And before I could say "fee-fi-fo-fum," pounced at me.

↔

Dark elves, the Sith of the fae world. Powerful, smart and mean, few cross swords, fists or pretty much anything with one of these guys and lives. And this one was going to crash into me. No human reflexes could stop that. But what I did have time to do was position my body so that when he tackled me, we would tumble out of the room.

My plan worked—sort of. He hit me so hard the breath was knocked out of me when we hit the back wall. I had just enough sense to move my head three inches so that the fist he followed up with hit the wall instead of me.

He pushed against me with bone-crushing strength. "Come on Jack," I said. "Any second now."

But Jack didn't move, and from the corner of my eye I could see him staring at us, his face wearing some sort of surprised shock.

"Jack," I cried out again, but the giant didn't move. The dark elf was grabbing at my shoulder, and I knew exactly what he was trying to do: turn me around and grab me by the neck so he could snap it.

I wasn't about to let that happen.

Interesting note: many Others do not share the same anatomical placements as humans. Many, but not all. Some, despite all their strength and abilities, are made up exactly like humans.

Elves were one of them.

Bringing my knee up as hard as I could, I kicked him where his anatomical weakness hung. He cringed in pain as his grip loosened. I kicked again and then a third time, when he punched me so hard in my side I saw stars.

Shake it off, girl, I thought, lowering an arm in case he wanted to hit me in the same spot again.

He pulled his fist back and was about to unleash another star-inspiring hit when someone came up from behind and hit him with a hockey stick.

Seeing that it was two against one (it should have been three with Jack, but the useless giant didn't move), the dark elf ran. I wanted to take a second to thank my savior, but he was already running after the elf. From the back, though, I could have sworn it was Justin.

Never mind that now, I thought, and had just started after him when a powerful hand grabbed my ankle.

I turned to see Jack holding my leg. Not crushing it, not trying to hurt me, but holding me back nonetheless. "Jack, what are you doing?" I said, and that's when things got really weird.

My vision blurred as the world around me started to spin. I felt like I was very drunk—worse than drunk—and as the world started to fade, I fell face-first onto the linoleum floor. I had just enough sense to see that Jack was also down.

Poison, I thought, and wondered if I would ever wake up again.

And as the world faded to black, the emptiness within me spoke up, asking a comforting question: *if you were to never wake, would that be so terrible?*

No, I thought as the peace that only a deep darkness can offer enveloped me. *No, it wouldn't be so terrible at all.*

End of Part 2

PART III
INTERMISSION

Have you ever loved someone so much that just the thought of them makes it hard to breathe? That's what was happening to Justin: he could barely breathe when he thought about Katrina dumping him.

She was going to leave him, and he was sure of it. His worst nightmare was coming true, except it wasn't a nightmare because he wasn't asleep. It was a nightmare that plagued him all the time, an obsession he harbored. And the weirdest part: it seemed the more he obsessed, the more he worried, the harder the snow fell. Like his heart somehow controlled the weather.

And as he watched Katrina hug her changeling roommate and run down the hill, his heart squeezed as if trying to expel every drop of blood in it, never to beat again. But it did beat, and with its thump, more snow fell.

Justin followed Kat as she ran, careful to keep a distance between them. The worst thing that could happen now was Kat catching him. He needed to be careful. After all, if Egya had noticed him following her, she could, too.

I need to be smart about this. And what was smart? Then it hit him.

Stop following her and talk to the changeling. She'd know something, perhaps provide a clue as to what the future had in store for them.

Running, he caught up with Deirdre, and before he could even say hello, she excitedly told him about her and Kat's Christmas plans.

An event. Three days in Douglas Hall. Three days over Christmas.

Three days when he would be worrying and suffering at home with his parents. He couldn't bear it, and then a thought struck him with such viciousness he almost questioned if it came from him. Sneak into Douglas Hall and join *her* for Christmas.

Now that was a plan. A plan with hope written all over it.

19

WAKING THE DEATH

*B*ut I did wake up. In the kitchen. With Jack.

Of all the mysteries that needed solving, how we wound up back here was a big one. How *I* got here, not so much. A strong eight-year-old could drag me across a football field. But Jack wasn't just a giant—he was a giant wearing a Gleipnir chain. Whoever dragged him back here had to be Hercules strong.

From where I lay on the cold linoleum floor, I could see that everyone else was down, too. Even Tiny.

I pulled myself onto a nearby chair and sat up way too fast. Whatever took me down wasn't totally gone, and I put my head down on the cool metal counter to stop the world from spinning. As soon as my flesh touched stainless steel, I felt better, as though its still surface was anchoring my spinning brain.

And from where I rested, I saw Snap, Crackle and Pop huddled together. They were also starting to stir, and Pop, his left hand expertly bandaged, gave me a tiny thumbs up.

Whatever had knocked us out wasn't poison. Poison strong enough to take down someone of Jack's size would have killed these little guys. It was something else. Magic, maybe? I didn't know, but that was also on my growing *What the Hell is Going On?* list.

One thing was clear: whoever roofied us probably wasn't one of the downed fae in this room. And I doubted it was the dark elf. If he'd known it would only be a matter of time until the drugs kicked in and I dropped, then why risk a fight?

Which meant there was someone else snowed in with us. Yay! More suspects.

We all slowly got to our feet, my head pounding worse than any hangover I've ever had the displeasure of living through.

"What—what happened?" Sarah asked.

"Welcome to the seedy underworld of college. We were roofied," I said. "But given we're all alive, I'm guessing the drugger didn't want us dead."

"And since we're all here," Remi said, "seems that exonerates us from being murderers. Even you, dear changeling."

Deirdre nodded her thanks, wincing in pain as she did.

If I didn't feel so lousy I might have said something snarky like, "No shit, Sherlock." But as it was, I was glad someone else was voicing their conclusions.

"Then there is an unknown quantity out there who killed Oighrig End?"

"A lone killer," Jarvis added. "Do you think he will strike at us next?"

Remi shook his head and immediately regretted it, rubbing his temples. Through the obvious disorientation, he did manage to get out, "I doubt it. The killer could have ended us all, and he—"

"Or *she* didn't," I added, not wanting to be sexist.

Remi sighed in agreement. "Or she didn't. All that said, I think we're safe."

"I don't know," I said, my head still on the counter. I was starting to feel better, but didn't want to risk any side effects from sitting up. "I hate to rain on your drug-fueled parade, but Jack here was a naughty, naughty boy." I pointed at the prone giant.

Jack growled in protest, and then grabbed his head in pain.

"Allow me, big fellow," Remi said, growling at me. "I believe that's giant for, 'Am not.' "

"OK, then defend this," I said, looking at the giant. "When that dark elf was trying to squeeze the life out of me, why didn't you do anything?"

"Dark elf?" Sarah said.

"Yeah, dark elf," I said. "And before any of you comes at me with an 'Are you sure?' or a 'How do you know?'—I know. I was attacked by a dark elf covered in human blood, I might add, and when he ran away and I tried to chase after him, Mr. Inactive Giant over there suddenly sprang to life and grabbed my ankle. I want to know why."

I purposefully didn't tell them about the guy with the hockey stick who had saved me. Despite who I thought it was, I knew better: Justin was with his parents, probably trashing me over cranberries and mash. It was the drugs coupled with who I had wanted to see that made my savior look like him.

So if it wasn't Justin who saved me, then it might be someone in this room. Which meant that one of us wasn't drugged and that person, or rather fae, may or may not be working with the dark elf.

GoneGodDamn it! Jessica Fletcher, I am not.

Either way, I was hoping that one of them would tip their hand and get me one step closer to figuring this whole thing out.

Deirdre stood to grab a chopping knife, and—less menacingly than usual—whispered, "Answer milady." She ground her teeth, holding back her pain.

I'd have thought a knife-wielding Deirdre would set these guys off, but no one moved. They just stared at the giant, who looked at his hands with heavy, sad eyes.

"Come on, dear fellow. Tell us."

Jack pursed his lips and grunted. Then his hands started moving. Sign language.

"Hold on, hold on. Does anyone understand him?" I asked.

Remi nodded. "I do." He crawled over to the giant. "My brother is deaf and my parents forced me to learn. A mistake on their part, if you ask me, because all it did was give us a secret language to play our foolish games with."

Aren't you full of surprises? I thought.

"I am indeed, young lady. I am indeed. Go on, Jack. Tell us."

The giant's hands started moving again, and as they did, Remi spoke. "He says he recognized the dark elf as ... as ..." Remi's voice faltered. "Are you sure?"

Jack nodded.

"But it can't be."

"What can't be?" I said.

"He says he saw Aelfric, but ..."

"Aelfric is dead," Sarah said. "Dead a long, long time ago."

I scanned the room and saw everyone was surprised by the name, even Deirdre. In fact, I seemed to be the only person in the room not wearing a look of utter shock on her face. I was feeling left out.

"Okey dokey," I said. "So, who's Aelfric?"

↔

"Aelfric, milady? He is the Elf King I told you about," Deirdre said.

"The one from King Orfeo's story," I said, forcing myself to my feet. If there was ever a time to be ready to duke it out, now was it. "The one you questioned Oighrig End about. The one that all of you are now shocked about."

"I know what you're thinking, and I will tell you right now that you are jumping to an assumption that simply is not true," Remi said, lifting his gloved hands as if in surrender.

"I don't know, sometimes assumptions tend to be pretty accurate. I'm starting to assume you all know each other and that somehow this Elf King, this ... this—"

"Aelfric the Great," Jarvis said in a mournful voice.

"—connects you all."

"But Aelfric was a king of the UnSeelie Court," Orange said, as though he were a child accusing his little brother of breaking the vase.

"And?" I said.

"And we are of the Seelie Court," the ugly elf said. "We would never—"

"I swear to the GoneGods, if the next word out of your lips is 'associate,' 'fraternize,' or 'hang out with,' I will punch you in the nose so hard your face will finally achieve the roundness your bald scalp so diligently aspires to."

"That, young lady, was a mouthful," Remi said, pulling out his phone. "And as for your earlier comments, I would like to say that you are not entirely wrong." He pulled up an email on his phone and handed it to me. "Please read."

Dear Sir,

You do not know me, but I come to you as I do not know where else to turn.

"This is sounding very Prince of Nigeria-*y*."

"Just read on," Remi said with impatience.

As you know, the departure of the gods has changed much, and while most Others have chosen to let go of their old conflicts to start over in this new GoneGod World, such peace is fragile.

I fear that the infamous Professor Oighrig End is preparing to write a book about certain events that may lead the fae courts to war. It has to do with the death of King Aelfric and the Seelie and UnSeelie courts' involvement in the Elf King's demise.

I have contacted several like-minded individuals in the hope of dissuading him from publishing this damning work, amongst whom are Orange Treener and Sarah Halvis at McGill University. They have agreed to host an event where individuals such as yourself can have unfettered access to the professor.

Please contact them for further information. We must do whatever we can to stop Professor Oighrig End from publishing such damning work. Should his thoughts be made public, they will sow further discontent between Others and humans and cause a war between the two fae courts that will cost many lives.

Your Friend,

Gergeion

"Gergeion … one of the three who couldn't make it because of the storm?" I asked, turning to Orange. "The reason why I could get tickets after all."

Orange nodded. "I'm afraid you were right. We tried to prevent your changeling friend from coming not because we are prejudiced, but because we feared she might be."

"Everyone in this room got a similar email from Gergeion because we all share one thing in common: we don't want to see war," Remi said.

"And that's why the ticket prices were so high," I said.

"Exactly," Sarah said. "As a university organization, we couldn't exclude anyone from joining—not without losing our university status. But we could price it high enough that the average student couldn't afford to attend."

"And I'm not average," I said.

"In so many ways," Remi said with a not *un*charming wink.

I considered apologizing for my earlier accusations of bias against Deirdre for being from the UnSeelie Court. But apologies, if they were coming, would have to wait until later.

"It seems Professor End has some proof that members of the Seelie Court let King Orfeo in so as to start a war between the UnSeelie Court and humans. A war that would weaken the UnSeelie Court and leave them vulnerable to invasion. Granted this happened hundreds of years ago, but fae have long memories, and many will take arms because of such revelations," Orange said, his voice high-pitched with frustration. "We were trying to convince him to stop the publication of his new book, and in doing so, prevent war."

"And when Oighrig End turned up dead, your plan kind of fell apart," I added.

"As you can imagine, the authorities discovering our plan would only accomplish two things. One, implicate us as murderers, and two, bring unwanted attention to Professor End's unpublished book."

I saw that. So it seemed this motley crew had good intentions. I looked around at Orange the elf and Sarah the halfling, Jack the giant and Freol, all of whom claimed to be Seelie Court members. But then there was Jarvis, and Snap, Crackle and Pop, who were obviously members of the UnSeelie Court.

And finally Remi the human, except I now had a feeling he wasn't who he claimed to be.

"Thank you," I said, "for telling the truth and letting me into your inner circle. I want to assure you that Deirdre and I agree with your motives. So can we agree to no more secrets?"

They nodded, but whether they meant it or not I couldn't tell.

"Good. Remi ..."

"Yes?"

"Your gloves, if you will."

Remi hesitated. "I already told you, I have a rare skin condition which I am terribly—"

"—self-conscious about. I know. But you also agreed to no more secrets. If you don't mind." I held out my hands.

Remi looked around before shaking his head. "You are a clever girl," he said, peeling off his gloves. "And what you are about to see will implicate me as the murderer, but I assure you I am not the murderer."

He took off his gloves and showed me two human-looking hands covered in dry green, blue, yellow and red blood.

I sucked in a breath. "You're a ly erg," I said. "I've heard of your kind, but never met one of you before. You're a fae soldier of the UnSeelie Court. Your kind is indistinguishable from human beings except for one strange trait: your hands become stained with the blood of anyone you've slain, like the handsy version of Redcap. Also kind of makes sense now that you'd call me 'young lady.' You're probably older than most mountains."

"I was a relatively young creation. Ten thousand years or so by human standards." Remi shrugged. "And as for me and Redcap, I personally would never compare myself to that goblin, but yes, we are both stained by those we kill. Him by his scalp, and me by my hands." Remi held his hands up before me. "See that green stain? Troll blood. One of those nasty fellows attacked me while on patrol before the gods left.

"This yellow"—he pointed at the upper joint of his thumb, which was a bright, lemon yellow—"a valkyrie who thought she could enter the UnSeelie Court to steal the Bone Flutes fashioned from Beowulf's skeleton. She killed two trolls trying to retrieve her coveted prize. I showed her that thieves and murderers would not be tolerated on my watch, and thus my thumb shall forever be the color of her blood. In fact, all these stains are in the service of my home, my gods, my king. And all before the gods left. Except this." He pointed at the lifeline on his right palm. It was stained red.

"Human blood," I said.

He pursed his lips and nodded. "There were moments during the first weeks following the gods' departure that I had to protect myself and those I love from enterprising human hunters."

That could be true, I thought. In the early days, just after the gods left, it seemed that any human with a gun deputized themselves and went after Others.

But then again, it could have been a lie, and the blood red stain could be because of Oighrig End.

"I am innocent," he said, as if reading my thoughts.

"I don't know," I said. "When the authorities eventually show up, I will have to tell them who and what you are."

I readied myself for an attack, but Remi just shook his head. "That will be a mistake," he growled, taking two steps in my direction. But he didn't take a third, instead clasping a hand over his mouth as if trying to push the words back down his throat. But they were out, so he said, "My apologies. Whatever knocked us out also put my manners to sleep. I see your predicament, and suspect I would do the same if I were in your shoes. Do as you must, young lady. No one here will try to stop you."

So Remi was willing to let me show them his blood-stained hands and a body. Either he was guilty and for some reason happy to face the consequences, or there was something else going on.

I'd barely had time to consider the possibilities when Sarah stood up and turned in the direction of my voice. "He's innocent."

"You can't see his hands. They're stained—"

"He's innocent. I know he is, because he was with me all evening."

↔

"So another little piece of truth comes out," I said. "You two are … what?"

"Engaged to be married," Remi said. "We will be the first of our kind. Seelie and UnSeelie Court members bound together by the sanctity of marriage."

"How *Romeo and Juliet* of you," I said.

"Turn him in and I shall confess to the murder, too. They can have two innocents in their cells, if they like."

"No," Orange said, "we're forgetting about the dark elf. You said he was covered in human blood."

"And apparently a ghost," I said, pointing at Jack. "Look, I don't know who's innocent and who's guilty. I don't know who's working with who, but a man was murdered, and we can't just say 'Forget it' because he happened to be an asshole. There's a body, and there will be an investigation."

"And if we just tell them about the dark elf, corroborate our stories, and—"

"A man died. A man died because—if I understand you all correctly —he wanted to tell the truth about some event that happened eight hundred years ago. That man did not have a chance to see the bigger impact of his book. He was not reasoned with so he could consider not publishing it. He was just murdered.

"But here's the thing: even if he had heard your arguments and chose to publish the book anyway, he still didn't deserve to die. No one deserves to die for wanting to share the truth."

I looked from person to person, and no one would meet my gaze.

It didn't matter. I believed what I'd said and would follow through. That was my truth. And if one of them came after me, if the dark elf chose to attack once more from the shadows, so be it. This was a truth I was willing to fight and die for.

"Good," I said. "Now if you don't mind, I think I've heard just about all the preaching I can stand. I'm going to bed, and I suggest we all do the same."

20

BEDTIME MUSINGS

*W*e still weren't sure who was working with whom, and we were only slightly closer to the truth, but we all retired to our rooms anyway. It had been a very long day.

Before I left, I grabbed the notes from all the interviews we did and, with only one copy of each, I was sure someone would protest. No one did. No one was interested in the interview notes. No one but me.

Deirdre asked to sleep with me, given her room was the scene of a murder. Once we were in the room, I dragged a couch to block our door. Deirdre, much stronger than me, lifted the oak wardrobe and set it atop the couch. "Just in case," she said.

Looking at her handiwork, I said, *"You're* my 'just in case.' "

With that we got into bed, and I went over the notes before finally giving up and throwing them to one side. I swear to the GoneGods, everyone's interviews were more 'How are you doing?' and less 'Where were you at the time of the murder?' Not to stereotype, but fae are the worst detectives.

Frustrated, confused and no closer to understanding what had happened, I tried to sleep. But the trouble with a murder and being roofied ... sleep doesn't come easy after all that. We lay awake, staring at the ceiling for a long time, neither of us speaking until Deirdre sighed. "We were all poisoned. Does that mean none of us is the killer?"

I thought about that for a long moment before shaking my head. "It might mean that, but then again, it might mean one or more of the group is working with someone else who's hiding in the shadows."

Deirdre hummed in agreement.

"Almost everyone there is hiding something."

"How so?" she asked.

"In a minute. First I want to ask you something. It might be the missing piece to the puzzle. Then again, it might mean nothing."

"Anything, milady."

"When we were examining Oighrig End's body, I saw you do that thing you do with your eyes when you're trying to keep a secret."

She did it again. "Do you think anyone noticed?"

I shook my head. "It was almost imperceptible. I only noticed because I've seen it before. But with that said, what did you see?"

"A thread from a thistle blade, milady."

"Thread? Thistle blade?"

She turned over and gave me a confused look, as if I must know what a thistle blade was. "A blade crafted from the barbs of a thistle flower. These threads are woven together so tightly that the blade is as sharp as a razor. Thistle blades are used when enacting revenge for a great crime."

Got to hand it to the fae—they had something for everything. "Deirdre, you mentioned that the blade was woven. But given how sharp the blade must be, I'm assuming tiny hands are needed to weave it?"

"Indeed, milady," Deirdre said solemnly.

"Abatwa-sized hands."

"Thistle blades are one of the crafts they are most revered for."

"I see. Given what happened to Pop, it might be the killer trying to tie up loose ends. You know, get rid of the guy who forged the murder weapon." I sighed as I thought about poor Pop and his missing leg.

Leg or no leg, I thought, *I guess no one is too small to be a suspect.*

"Or too big," she said to my out-loud thought. She reached down and touched her bruised ankle.

Or too close to me, I thought (in my head).

"Deirdre," I said, "you're my friend and I'll defend you until kingdom come."

"I think kingdom came," she said with a smile.

"Joke?"

"Joke."

"Not bad, my changeling friend, not bad. But what I want to ask you—need to ask you—comes from a place of love and respect. And whatever the answer, I swear I will never betray you."

"You wish to know if I am the one who ended Oighrig End?"

I nodded.

"Milady, I have sworn to you my sword arm and heart. There is nothing I would not tell you."

"Good," I said, looking into her eyes. She didn't speak. "And?" I said.

"And what, milady? If I had wanted to kill Oighrig End, I would have had to request your permission first. But I did not request, nor did you command. My hand had nothing to do with his death."

Of course, I thought. I wasn't thinking this all through. By giving me her sword arm, she had basically handed over all free will when it came to fighting, maiming and killing. The only way she could be responsible for killing Professor End was if I had told her to, making me just as much the murderer as her. More so, even.

"OK," I said, "so we can rule you out. Can we rule anyone else out?"

Deirdre gave me a confused look. "Milady, I was led to believe that everyone was innocent. After all, we were all drugged, you have personally seen a dark elf, and then there is the matter of that email Remi LaChance showed you."

I shook my head. "I'm afraid none of that exonerates anyone."

Now it was Deirdre's turn to give me a curious look.

"OK, let's take this one by one. Being drugged. I didn't mention this before because I was hoping someone would slip up, but it wasn't just the dark elf, Jack and me. There was someone else."

"Who?"

"I don't know, but when the dark elf was squeezing the life out of me, someone came to my rescue, which means there are either two people running loose in the building and they aren't working together, which is an unlikely scenario, or one of them pretended to be drugged, and when the other player—this dark elf wildcard—attacked, their better nature came out and they saved me."

The changeling shook her head. "Milady, I am grateful there is another amongst us who is fighting for your safety."

"Yeah, but—"

"That aside," Deirdre said, interrupting me in a manner uncharacteristic for her, "I have never known you to be so suspicious. I believe all known individuals to be innocent, and I agree with your theory that there are two people hiding amongst us who are working together. But my reasoning is different than yours."

As much as I like being right, I wanted to follow her logic through. "OK, I'll bite … how so?"

"You saw the wounds on Oighrig End. They were inconsistent and from multiple angles, as if whoever stabbed him did so with one hand, then switched hands and continued stabbing. That suggests that two conspirators working together to end End is far more likely."

"And one tried to kill me while the other saved me?"

"Why not? Two conspirators may share a common enemy in Professor End, but not in you. Dark elves are not known for their restraint, and when he attacked you, the other simply stepped in to avoid compounding the tragedy with the death of an innocent."

I hadn't considered that. Not all murderers were created equal, and it was possible that one was willing to kill again and again to preserve their anonymity, while the other refused to cross that line. "OK," I said, "let's say you're right about that. What about Jack stopping me from chasing the dark elf?"

"Have you considered that the giant may have been trying to save your life?"

I raised a doubtful eyebrow.

"Think about it. He could not help you battle this dark elf, and knew you were outmatched. He understood that if you chased after the dark elf it might lead to your death, so he stopped you from doing so."

"True," I said. "And the dark elf's co-conspirator might have saved me when I accidently stumbled upon his hiding place. He may think twice about saving me again when I actively chase them. So Jack was trying to save me."

"Perhaps. But then again, perhaps not."

"So I may or may not owe him an apology," I said. "Then there's the matter of Jack really thinking the dark elf is King Aelfric."

Deirdre shook her head. "I have considered this point again and again, and I believe it to be glamor. The dark elf knew Jack would not raise a hand against his former king, and made his appearance resemble the giant's dead king."

"I agree. A trick is far more believable than the elf returning from the dead. But none of that matters. I still think one or more of them is lying."

"Why? When you consider the email, it exonerates them all."

"It's precisely because of the email that I still have my doubts."

Deirdre tilted her head.

"Remi showed me the email on his web browser."

"I do not follow, milady."

"Web browsers on smart phones tend to refresh every time you open them. We don't have access to the internet, which means that he either took a screenshot of the email—something you wouldn't do unless you expected to be without internet—or he forged it to throw me off."

"Oh," Deirdre said, taking my word for it. She wasn't one for technology, and frequently asked me questions even a technically challenged grandmother would roll her eyes at.

"So that's why I want to know who we can rule out."

Deirdre gave me a mournful look. This investigation was far from over. "Sadly, because the weapon is a thistle blade, both Jarvis and the abatwas could be responsible."

"The abatwas? Aren't they too … you know," I gave her the universal gesture for *super-duper tiny*.

She gave me an admonishing look and I remembered how easily they'd carried the chairs and speakers. They were strong, and if they worked together, they could have easily killed Professor End.

"OK," I said, "so they're suspects. What about Jack?"

"A warrior who carries the Gleipnir chain. If his history intersects with Oighrig End's, or if he is beholden to one whose does …"

"So the giant is in. What about the rest?"

"The elf and halfling do not seem to have any motivations or clues against them, but that does not mean innocence. And as for the human soldier, he did question Oighrig End with vigor bordering on anger. But again, there are no clues pointing to his hand in this."

"So they're in, too. Which only leaves us Freol?"

She shrugged.

Freol still hadn't said a word to me. In fact, he still hadn't met my eyes. The guy was a bit creepy—especially in that suit.

"Can't discount him, either. So basically everyone is a suspect. And because of what happened earlier, everyone's also innocent. In other words, we have no idea who was and wasn't involved."

"That's not true. We know we weren't a part of this, but that's about it."

"True," I said, "but there's more at play than a single murderer in our midst."

"Such as, milady?"

"Nightmares. When I was asleep, I dreamt of something so vivid it had to be a memory. But it wasn't mine. And I can't even remember what happened in it—only the feeling it gave me."

Deirdre gave me a grave look. "A nightmare? When did this happen, milady?"

"Just before you discovered Oighrig End's body."

Deirdre pursed her lips. "Do you remember anything about that dream?"

I shook my head. "All I remember is I was seeing something from the eyes of another. And what I saw left me with this terrible feeling.

116

But that's not all … I'm seeing things. When that dark elf was stran-
gling me, I thought I saw Justin. He was the one who hit the elf with
the hockey stick. Saved me. But it couldn't be him. He's home with his
parents, and—"

The thought of Justin on top of everything else that was happening
—the murder, the fights, the emptiness inside me—was just too much.
And as far as seeing him? I think I just *wanted* to see him. Wanted to be
saved by him.

Deirdre must have seen the distress on my face, because she put a
cool hand on my chest just above my heart. In a way, that gesture was
a fae hug. It was her way of telling me that she was here for me, no
matter what.

"Thank you, Deirdre, but I'll be OK," I said, touching her hand.
"Really, I will. I think it was just the lack of oxygen and the fact that I
wanted to see Justin. We ended our last talk on such horrible terms,
and I've been so—"

I thought about telling Deirdre about the emptiness, but decided
not to. She had just lost her hero, and as much as I was sure we were
no longer in harm's way, it didn't change that we were stuck in a
building with a murderer on the loose.

Deirdre had been serious when she offered me so much of her, and
she would make my emptiness the top-priority on her *To-Do* list. But
that could wait until we were out of this place.

So instead of opening up to my friend, I said, "It's nothing. I'm just
tired. Let's sleep."

Deirdre gave me a long, hard look, her hand still on my chest.
"Very well, milady. We are safe in here, and you are safe with me."

"Thank you," I said, turning around to sleep.

↔

As much as I wanted to sleep, I was afraid of having another nightmare. Even as an observer, the last one was awful. I wished I could remember any details about it, but all I really remembered was the horrible feeling when I woke. That, and death.

It took what felt like an eternity for sleep to come. I must have tossed and turned for an hour before my fears finally succumbed to my exhaustion.

My foolish fears ... they should have fought harder.

The dream that came was my worst nightmare wrapped in a duvet of horrible. It started pleasant enough: I was in bed, and Justin was rubbing my back the way he did. He was humming something, and although I couldn't make out the tune it filled me with a sense of peace. This was nice. This was good.

But the rubbing became harder, started to hurt. I turned to ask Justin to relax, but instead of seeing my beautiful, intact boyfriend with the impossibly beautiful eyes and perfect hair, I saw a bald, hollow-eyed Justin.

He looked like he had died a year ago and was only now returning, half-decomposed. I screamed, not that Justin noticed; he continued humming, but his song no longer soothed me.

"I want you to know that I don't blame you," he said between notes. "You are trying to make up for all the wrong you've done in your long, long life, and what happened isn't your fault. It's just that death follows you."

Justin sat up and showed me his arms. Much of the flesh had left them, but enough remained for me to see the long slits from his wrists to his elbows.

The word "suicide" tumbled out, and my hand went to my mouth as if to hold the word back, and when it failed to do so, to capture it before it traveled too far.

Justin nodded. "I couldn't live without you. When you left me, rather than be alone, I took the coward's way out."

"We ... we ... are still—"

"Are we?" he said in a harsh tone. "Are we? Or are you gathering the courage to say goodbye? Biding your time while I spend a week in hell waiting for you to decide what will happen to us, not caring what I want? What I need!"

Justin's corpse sat up, his brittle bones snapping with the effort. His movement was so sudden, so violent that I moved away from him, falling on the floor as I did.

When I stood, I saw through tear-filled eyes that he had snapped his spine. His torso had separated from his legs.

He looked down at his detached legs before turning to me. "You did this! You selfish bitch—you did this!"

I screamed, and I think I would have continued screaming had a harsh, hard hand not slapped my face. Once, then again. And on the third slap, I turned to see Deirdre standing next to me. "Milady," she said, "you are safe, milady. Safe with me."

It took a few seconds before I realized I was still in bed. No Justin, no bones or taut skin stretched over bones. Just my friend and me.

I got up, got away from the bed. I didn't care if it was just a dream. I didn't care that I knew Justin was home with his family, that he was safe, and that we were still together.

That he was still alive.

The dream felt real. More than *felt* real ... as far as I was concerned, it *was* real.

I went to the door and tried to get out, but even with all the adrenaline pumping through my body, I wasn't strong enough to move the wardrobe. Not that it stopped me from trying. I pawed at the damn thing, desperate to get away, my tears equal parts frustration and despair. I might have continued that way all night had Deirdre not picked up the wardrobe and moved it.

With it gone, I pulled at the couch, unlocked the door and left the room. I had no idea where I was going. My only thoughts were of getting away.

I walked downstairs. With every step I took away from the room, I calmed little by little. By the time I made it to the ground floor, I had found myself again.

Good, I thought, taking a deep breath and wiping away tears. *Better.*

Much better. I turned to see Deirdre behind me, her face a mixture of fear and concern.

"Better," I whispered. Then I remembered how vivid the dream was, and I couldn't face going back upstairs. Besides, I'd never fall asleep again tonight—not after that. "I just can't go back into that room. I need to be somewhere else."

Deirdre put a hand on her chest, the fae's way of saying *As you wish*, and she gestured toward the conference room. "Perhaps you will find peace there."

I nodded. As we drew closer to the unlit room, we heard voices.

As distressed as I was, we were still trapped in a building with a murderer. I placed a finger over my lips and the two of us took another step forward, listening.

"If this is some kind of cruel joke or trick, I swear on my father's name I will end you." It was Sarah's voice.

"No trick, my little fairy angel—"

"Don't you dare call me that. Only he can call me that. Only he …"

"But it's me, my darling Sonia."

Sonia? I thought her name was Sarah. I looked at Deirdre, whose eyes widened at the mention of the name.

"No," she said, "you're dead. They told me you're dead."

"Funny," the voice said, "they said the same thing to me about you. It seems we have both been lied to."

"If it is really you, and not a trick or a glamor, prove it."

"Very well," the voice said. "Do you remember the night of the attack, when the barguests came? Do you remember what we were playing?"

"Checkers. Well, what we called checkers then."

"Do you remember the score?"

"Yes," she said, her voice sharp, afraid.

"Seven games to one. In your favor."

Sarah—or was it Sonia?—let out a sharp wail that could only come from one truly in pain. "This is a trick. A lie. A lie. You lie!"

"No, my sweet fairy angel, it is me. I swear it. It's me."

"Let me go. Let me—"

Sneaking around or not, I barged into the room, turning on the lights as I did. There I saw the dark elf reaching for Sarah as the halfling pulled back, desperate to get away.

That was all I needed to see. I tumbled toward the dark elf, planning to get behind him and punch him in the back of neck.

You know what they say about plans: you make 'em, and dark elves laugh.

And that was literally what he did. He laughed as he turned around with the kind of speed I didn't think possible and backhanded me across the room.

21

DARK ELVES AND KIDNAPPING PAPAS

The dark elf's backhand sent me flying toward the wall with such speed and ferocity that it could well have broken my back had Deirdre not caught me mid-flight.

Putting me down, she looked at the dark elf and I swear I saw her grow in size as she huffed and growled, preparing for battle. "You dare," she said, pointing her finger at the elf. She charged at him, swinging her fist.

He ducked under and counter-punched, but Deirdre was ready, deflecting the blow with a downward swing of her arm.

"I dare," he said, his voice commanding and confident. "I am not the one who attacks their king."

"There are no more kings," Deirdre said, grabbing a chair and throwing it at him. "No more queens, no more gods, no more UnSeelie Court." With each statement she threw another chair, and although he deflected them easily, I saw what she was doing: keeping him off balance and pushing him toward me. "Everything we once knew is gone. We have been abandoned. Abandoned on this mortal plane."

"Don't be foolish. Oberon and Titania would never leave us. They would—"

I kicked him in the back of the knee and as he went down, Deirdre tackled him, wrapping her powerful arms around his body.

"What are you doing?" he cried out.

Grabbing his legs, I held them together so he couldn't kick his way out. "Grappling an asshole," I said.

"I am your king," he screamed at Deirdre.

"You are, my lord, but I have sworn my sword arm and heart to her," Deirdre said, but she said it in the same tone she used when she wasn't sure about human etiquette. Things like: 'Can I cut in line?' 'Can I scream for the waiter's attention?' 'Can I punch the boy staring at my butt?'

Before they could work out the standards of fae hierarchy, a boom came from the door and broken stone flew into the room. I turned to see Jack pushing through, ripping the door frame out of the wall. He stopped when he saw who we were grappling with, neither helping nor hindering us.

Behind him I heard footsteps as Orange, Remi and Jarvis ran in. One of them said, "King Aelfric," and whether it was Jarvis or Remi I could not tell.

Out of breath, Remi went to Sarah. "My darling, are you harmed?"

"No," she said, "I'm not. Who … who is that?" She pointed in our direction, where we were still wrestling with the dark elf. I'd fought strong before, but never this strong. I could see on Deirdre's face that it took everything she had to hold him down.

Remi turned to us. "I can tell you who it looks like."

The dark elf stopped struggling and said, "My daughter Sonia—please, search yourself. You know it is me."

The halfling lifted a regal hand, demanding silence. The dark elf, Deirdre and me—hell, everyone in the room—shut the hell up.

"I know you said something to me," she said, "just before I lost my sight. I was crying, afraid that without sight I wouldn't be able to find you again. You said I always would, because you would come to my side and whisper a secret word only we knew. Tell me that word now, or I swear I will command Jack and Remi to rip you apart. Slowly."

Daaaamn! The halfling got bite, I thought.

"They would never hurt their king," the dark elf said.

In answer, Jack pounded his fists together and Remi removed his gloves. It was clear where their loyalties lay.

"Good," the dark elf said, no longer trying to break free. Rather than being intimidated by Jack and Remi, he seemed pleased. Relieved, even. He looked at the giant and ly erg. "I am so grateful for your loyalty, that she had the two of you in my absence." He looked at Sarah, or Sonia, or whoever she was. "I … I have missed so much. I have not had the pleasure of seeing you turn from a girl into the beautiful woman you are today. You look so much like your mother. So much so that it was I who thought he'd seen a ghost."

"Enough!" the halfling screamed. "Tell me the word, or death."

"Very well, but there is one problem. I swore to you that day I would never share that word with anyone but you."

"Oh, give me a break," I said. "Surely there's a break clause. As in, me happily breaking your legs."

"Silence, vampire," the dark elf scoffed.

"I'm not … not a vampire."

"Lie to yourself if you wish, but a vampire dressed in human clothing is still a vampire."

I didn't know how he knew, but I squeezed his legs together in response.

He winced in pain before looking at the halfling. "I swore to you, made an oath. I cannot break it."

Fae and their oaths. But he was right: if he swore to never share the word with anyone but her, then there wasn't a torture technique, a truth serum or a confession spell in this universe or any other that would get him to talk.

A long silence elapsed until Sarah finally spoke. "Let him go."

"What? No, my darling. He is just trying to get close to you so that he may—"

"Let him go," she said in the commanding tone the dark elf had used earlier.

Deirdre looked at me and nodded. We let go.

Free of us, the dark elf pulled himself from the floor and slowly approached Sarah.

"If you hurt her," Remi said, putting a hand on his chest as he drew close to Sarah.

"So now it is to you that I make this oath, my Rem-ii," he said, pronouncing the ly erg's name with a heavy fae accent. "My faithful soldier and friend, I will never hurt the halfling whom you hold so dear."

Remi's eyes widened. He removed his hand from his chest.

The Elf King took another two steps toward Sarah. Standing before her, he brushed back her long amber hair before leaning in close and whispering a word into her ear.

The halfling placed a trembling hand over her mouth, and a tear that had escaped her eye rolled over her fingers. In a voice that belonged more to a child than a fully grown halfling princess, she returned his word with a lone word of her own. "Father?"

2 2
DEATH DOES NOT BECOME HIM

*I*t's not every day your father returns from the dead. Believe me, I know. My mother returned from the dead (largely because I turned her into a vampire three hundred years ago) and that was a shock. But then again, I didn't have the best relationship with her.

Judging by the halfling's tears, I guessed that wasn't the case for her. This grown young lady fell into her father's embrace like a toddler who knows that the safest and most loving place to be is in your parents' arms. If she was conscious of us watching her, she made no show of it as she cried with tears she must have saved just for him through all these centuries.

I would later learn that her father had died when she was eight, and the tears she cried that night in Douglas Hall's lecture room were for every scraped elbow, head bump and bruised knee he wasn't there to make better.

Her tears were for every maypole game lost, for every missed father-daughter dance, for every bad dream he wasn't there to comfort her after.

Her tears were for all the victories, too: every game won, every A+ earned, every moment she had triumphed.

Her tears were for all the little moments that make up a childhood.

She fell into his arms, allowing him to envelop her as though to make up for it all. An impossible task, but one that both of them were willing to take on.

As they cried, he hummed in that way only the fae are capable of, and what I felt there was an unfaltering, unwavering love. This dark elf, this king, would die for her. He *did* die for her. And whether by magic or time or the departure of the gods or just sheer willpower, he came back from the dead to be with her one more time.

We let them have their time, slowly departing from the conference room to the kitchen while they celebrated their tearful reunion.

↔

That night, no one spoke for a long time in the kitchen. No one said anything as we loitered around the room's metal tables and near its stainless steel refrigerators, ovens and stoves.

No one spoke, but in our silence, we said volumes of soundless words. It started with Orange removing his wig, revealing his red scalp. With it gone, the ugly elf's features began to change and he morphed into a goblin. *Magic*, I thought. *Probably the wig possesses a minor glam that allowed this algae-colored goblin to look like a human flesh-colored elf.*

But his metamorphosis also revealed something else: he wasn't Orange the elf, and never had been. His red scalp told us who he really was.

Next was Jarvis. He removed his hat and valet coat. There was no magical transformation, no trow becoming something else. But still he changed, a bright smile adorning his face. Jarvis—or whatever his real name was—reached for Orange's hand and once they were together, they both wore a look of relief, as if the simple act of their hands touching made everything right in this world.

United, they both pulled out pendants from their pockets and pinned them to their shirts. The artistry was incredible, and the pendent that was no more than three inches in length looked like it was built from a thousand tiny leaves woven together.

Deirdre's eyes widened in recognition, not because she didn't approve of a trow and goblin union, but because their reunion confirmed who they really were. "Redcap and Krelis," she said.

The two, still hand in hand, nodded, placing their free hands over their hearts—the UnSeelie Court salute.

Remi too removed his disguise, taking off his gloves and tossing them in the garbage before putting on the same pendant as Orange and Jarvis ... or rather, Redcap and Krelis. He looked at his multicolored palms, a rainbow of blood, all creatures felled by his hands. He rubbed the red stain on his palm like he was trying to remove it.

Jack too transformed. While his appearance stayed the same, he reached into his pockets and pulled out two shackles that he put around his wrists. As soon as the metal braces locked, chains grew out of them and as they lengthened, he wrapped them around his wrists, forearms and biceps until his arms looked they were made of chain-linked metal. That done, he put on the same pendant.

"Jack-in-Chains," Deirdre said, saluting him in their fae way before bowing. Changelings only bow when presenting themselves to their superiors, which meant that Jack-in-Chains wasn't just a giant ... he was a military general of the UnSeelie Court.

Even Tiny had left his master's side to be with us in the kitchen. Sitting there, I saw the dog's uncomprehending gaze replaced by intelligent, observant eyes. I had spent enough time among the fae to know what he was: a barguest, the fabled black dog of the UnSeelie Court. Intelligent, vicious and GoneGodDamn loyal to whomever they pledge their allegiance to.

Tiny wasn't Sarah's Seeing Eye dog; he was her bodyguard.

Only Freol didn't move, staring with an impassive gaze at the fae in the room.

"So," I said, "I guess there's a lot you've been hiding."

"I fear we have," Remi said, "and before you ask the million questions I am sure you have, perhaps we can show you something."

↔

Remi removed his pendant and blew into it. So did the others. A mist of glitter flew out of them, combining in the center of the room to form a globe filled with a million tiny flickering bugs.

"Beag solas, the Unseelie version of fireflies. They have been trained to tell a story. A story we all have watched over and over to remind ourselves of our purpose, and why we exist," Remi said, running his hands through the golden mist.

The globe began to form detailed images that few mortal hands could paint. The fae began to hum, imbuing the evolving light with emotion.

And in this way, the story began to unfold.

23
CONNECTING THE FIREFLY DOTS

hree figures—a man, woman and child—stood by a golden river. The details in the morphing image were so precise that I immediately recognized Aelfric, and Sonia as a young child.

The third figure was a woman with long amber hair cascading over her shoulders and down her figure. From the way they walked hand in hand, I knew this third figure had to be Heurodis.

The three of them were so happy, like I was watching the happily ever after promised in so many fairy tales.

But soon that happiness became something else. The fireflies traded their brilliance for something darker, something more sinister. Another scene unfolded.

In it, Aelfric and a very young Sonia—maybe four or five—were camping, and while this scene had no words, I knew this was something father and daughter often enjoyed doing together. Even though this was a serene scene, the fae humming told me something horrible was about to happen.

The scene flew away like glitter in a wind tunnel, and we were in a castle. Heurodis was combing her hair in what must have been her bedroom when Jack-in-Chains came crashing through the door. Well, crashing implies he pushed his way in. It was more like some incredible force pushed him in, if pushing mimicked the force of a train plowing through a cow.

Jack, clearly hurt, rose to his feet and attacked the force that had pushed him aside like one might toss an annoying cat. I couldn't see who or what was behind that blow—the fireflies didn't band together to create an image of what it could be—but from the way Heurodis backed away, and the single-minded focus of Jack's ineffectual attempts to overpower it, the source was clear.

A single figure stood in the middle of the room.

The giant leapt forward, bringing down two balled fists on the invisible figure. The blow was so powerful that the fireflies scattered like dust before reassembling into a scene that must have been hours later.

There stood a wounded Jack, his left arm in a sling. He was standing guard over Heurodis's unmoving body as Aelfric and Sonia lamented their loss.

Heurodis was dead.

The scene morphed. A war council had convened, and Aelfric sat on the throne. Several fae below were screaming for war—Remi amongst them—while others counselled against it. Both groups were yelling at each other and at the Elf King, who sat impassive. This went on for a long while before Aelfric lifted a silent hand, his decision finally made.

There would be no attack on the human domain, no revenge sought for this kingdom's loss.

They would do nothing.

Aelfric left the room as his council continued to shout and scream, desperate that this insult to their kingdom be answered.

The fireflies' glow dimmed and brightened, dimmed and brightened with the passage of time. Seasons came and went, trees grew and were felled before the bio-luminant, magical bugs settled on another time and place.

Sonia, now eight or nine, lived in a cabin in the woods. Inside was modest, a home well taken care of, well-loved, but also devoid of any living soul except Sonia.

She lived there alone.

She was seated on the porch, her excitement palpable. I saw a girl who wanted nothing more than to run up the path leading to the cabin. And she would have, but her caretakers held her back with squeaked admonishments. My gaze focused on the spot next to Sonia, which magnified (the fae equivalent of spreading apart thumb and finger on an iPad, except this three-dimensional display was far more advanced than anything Apple ever came up with) to reveal three abatwas sitting next to her: Snap, Crackle and Pop.

So Sonia wasn't alone. She had three loving, capable caretakers with her. Granted, they were loving, capable and *watch where you step* tiny caretakers, but caretakers nonetheless.

Sonia stared up the path until a figure came over the hilltop. She burst toward him, and there wasn't a force in this world or any other that could have stopped her.

The figure dismounted his steed and ran toward her, and with every step the fireflies revealed more details of who he was: King Aelfric.

The halfling jumped into her father's arms and the two of them hugged for a long time, the same sort of embrace they had shared in the conference room.

Seeing that made two things very apparent. First, that King Aelfric worried for his daughter's safety and hid her in the forest, away from the UnSeelie Court and his enemies who hid in the shadows.

Second, they hugged that way because their relationship would soon end. This was the beginning of that end, and my heart thumped as I realized I would soon see what had separated them.

In moments like this, as much as you anticipate the horror to come, as much as you try to will it away, fighting the inevitable is like trying to hold back a ferocious tide.

Father and daughter sat together talking, laughing. They played a game of checkers as the sun continued its climb. Morning became afternoon, and afternoon became dusk.

Dusk became night.

That was when the monsters appeared.

Several creatures attacked the cabin. Even King Aelfric, a force of unimaginable power, couldn't be everywhere to protect his daughter. Felling beast after beast with his sword, he screamed for her to run.

And the halfling child did as her father commanded. She ran into the dark forest surrounding her home. She ran and ran and ran.

Even though the fireflies didn't show me what she was thinking or unveil her feelings, I knew she was terrified. Perhaps this was because of the fae humming, but I didn't think so.

Because as much as their song imbued this horrific scene with emotion, I knew what she was afraid of, and it wasn't the monsters.

She feared that her father no longer breathed, that one of the beasts had got the best of him and left his body atop a patch of dirt in front of the cabin with his throat ripped out.

A fate worse than death. More than that: his death was her death. And as fear so often does, it lied to her, telling her that these weren't her worst nightmares playing macabre games with her mind, but the truth.

Her father was dead. She was certain.

And because his death meant she could no longer live, she stopped running and waited for the monsters to come and consume her, too. She waited for death and the dreams that follow.

But death is a cruel bitch; she torments her prey. As the monsters surrounded her, they did not attack.

She didn't know this then, but they did not attack because she stood in a clearing, daring them to come forth. They interpreted her acceptance of the death they brought as a trap. They hesitated. They were afraid.

The monsters were afraid of her.

Sonia picked up a rock and tossed it at them. Her aim was true and it hit one of the barguests between its eyes. The rock did little damage, more an insult than a blow, but it did the trick: the assaulted beast lunged forward, trap or no trap, to end the little girl.

As it leapt into the air, Sonia lifted her thistle blade that the abatwas had constructed just for such a moment. And with it she stabbed deep into the barguest's neck.

The barguest bit down on her shoulder, and the two became locked in death's embrace. Her blade bore down on the beast, and its fangs ripped her flesh.

One of them would have to give, and soon it was a matter of will. Sonia stabbed it again and again, and soon the contest ended. Sonia was the victor, and the barguest was dead.

But Sonia was mortally wounded.

So be it. Sonia stood and gestured for the next beast. Three of them answered her call. They leapt into the air, and all three died before touching the ground.

There stood King Aelfric with his sword, dispatching the beasts in a fury that would have frightened Oberon and Titania into groveling submission.

The remaining beasts, seeing that they would not claim their victim this day, fled.

King Aelfric embraced his bleeding daughter, showering her with kisses and tears.

She was dying, and this was something the king would not accept. Using his magic and strength, he carried her home to the UnSeelie Court. From the fireflies' brutal portrayal, I watched as three days and three nights passed.

I watched as Sonia's wound became infected and her eyesight left her.

I watched as a father, desperate to save his little girl, ran through the forest.

Three days and three nights, and they were home. King Aelfric handed his daughter over to the healers and waited.

And waited.

And waited … until finally a healer returned, shaking her head.

I did not know what was said. But I did know how he expressed his grief. With blood and pain.

In a brilliant flash we were on the mortal plane, at the walls of King Orfeo's castle. The fury of my dream came back to me as Aelfric killed human guard after human soldier. This was the battle I had watched unfold before me only a night ago.

The Elf King killed them all, every last soldier, before entering Orfeo's chambers. The human king was on his knees, begging for forgiveness, and Aelfric did the last thing I expected of him. He granted it.

King Aelfric did not end Orfeo, but instead looked at the human for a long, long time before leaving the mortal king unharmed.

That was where the scene ended, the fireflies returning to their pendants, the once radiant room darkened by their departure.

↔

With all that done, Remi sighed. "Now that you have some understanding, I am sure you still have a million questions. We are pleased to answer them all as best we can."

24

TYING UP LOOSE ENDS

"Why didn't he kill Orfeo and complete his revenge?"

"That is a question I have asked myself a thousand times. We all have. I guess he didn't want to start a war between fae and humans. Or maybe his senses returned to him and the horror of all the death caught up to him. Whatever his reasons were, I suspect we can now ask him," Remi said.

"And what is your role in all of this? Let me guess, you're all from the UnSeelie Court, and more specifically, served King Aelfric," I said, my gaze scanning each of them.

They all nodded, evidently no longer wishing to hide anything.

"And Sarah, or Sonia—"

"Sonia," Remi clarified.

"She is the halfling child in the story. A child who is now all grown up."

"Yes," Remi said.

"But I thought she died."

"She did," Remi said. "Dead as can be in a world with magic, but she came back. We don't know why or how, but again, we have our theories," he said, pointing at the solemn, silent Other called Freol. "We think it is because of him. Make no mistake, we did not expect him to show up yesterday. He was a surprise, to say the least. But then again, it is always a surprise when Ankou appears."

"Ankou?" Deirdre said. As the shock of who this black-suited Other was subsided and she got ahold of herself, Deirdre dropped to her knees, signing three intersecting diamonds on her forehead—the fae symbol for worship.

Whereas Deirdre's murmuring of the name 'Ankou' was filled with awe and respect, my tone was half-confused, half-*will someone clue me in?* "Ankou? Who is that?"

"Our grim reaper," Remi said, sighing. "He only shows up when a great death is about to happened. Except for that one moment when he showed up, and Sonia rose from the dead. It was so unheard of that we all swore never to speak of this until—well, now." Remi walked over to the fae reaper. "If only you would grace us with a few words so that we may know why you are here."

Ankou didn't answer, his face impassive and unmoving, revealing nothing. *This guy should play poker*, I thought. As in Texas hold 'em, high stakes, everything-on-the-line kind of poker.

Remi chuckled. "Can you at least tell me if you are here for me?"

Nothing. With that, Remi sighed. "He's here for one of us, maybe all of us. That's what we thought, but now that King Aelfric is here, I'm wondering if he's returned to play his back-from-the-dead trick again."

"Yeah," I said, as the gravity of the situation came crushing down on me. A literal *let me show you to your death* reaper was in the room with us—had been in the room with us—and now a dead king was back and we were snowed in, unable to escape. This situation had the endings of *Hamlet*, *Romeo and Juliet* and *Othello* wrapped in one written all over it.

I took a deep breath. "So if he's not Freol, but rather Ankou the friggin' Reaper ... who the hell are the rest of you?"

"Allow me to properly introduce myself. I am the dreaded Redcap," Orange said, throwing away the wig in his hand. He seemed happy to be rid of it; he rubbed his hands over his bald head.

"I would say it's a pleasure, but I've heard all about you," I said.

"Mostly exaggerations," he said. "Mostly."

"And Krelis here."

"My husband."

"As you are mine," Krelis said, facing Redcap. "Then, now and here."

" 'Then, now, here,' " I repeated. "Let me guess, when Redcap was accused of letting King Orfeo in, you were both driven from your home."

"Yes," Redcap said. "I had a choice: stay and die, or flee and live."

"And you, Krelis? What choice were you given?"

"I fear I am not much for anything other than drinking and—"

"And singing and dancing and making all things right in the world. At least in my world."

If I didn't know this before, I knew it then: trows can blush and goblins can be romantic. I swooned in jealousy over the obvious love they had for one another.

Krelis cleared his throat. "I stayed behind, telling everyone who came to our home looking for him that the dreaded Redcap had killed himself in shame."

"And I went into hiding for a thousand years, only now daring to show myself," Redcap said.

I got it. The gods may have been gone, and the amnesty program may have been in place, but it didn't change that many members of the UnSeelie Court wanted revenge for the death of their king. Amnesty was about forgiving the sins of the past, not forgetting them. Besides it was a government program—a *human* government program —and most Others didn't really go for the whole mortal law thing. "And you, Jack-in-Chains. You wear your Gleipnir chain as penance for failing to save Heurodis."

Remi walked over to Jack-in-Chains and made a gesture that left the giant smiling. "My brother here, he did everything in his power to protect Heurodis, but King Orfeo possessed a great magic that would have overpowered Oberon himself. Her death was not his fault … not that he would ever admit as much."

Remi hopped onto the table and, now only slightly taller than his giant brother, gave Jack a solemn, healing kiss on the forehead.

"And despite losing his wife, King Aelfric did not attack the human world. Not then, at least."

"He knew a war between fae and humans would not end well," the ly erg said.

"And who are you?" I asked Remi.

The soldier snapped his feet together and gave me a human salute. "I am Remi LaChance now, but I was Rem-ii Ly Erg, captain of King Aelfric's guard."

"And the abatwas—Snap, Crackle and Pop?"

"You saw them in the fireflies' dance. For all practical purposes, they were Sonia's mother, father and fun uncle rolled into one. The night of the attack—the night she died—was their worst nightmare come true. And even despite Sonia's resurrection, they have a score to settle."

Remi's words were accented with several high-pitched squeals as the abatwas raised their fists in exaggerated anger.

I guess when you're that small, you need to exaggerate everything just to be heard.

"And this big guy," I said, pointing at Tiny the barguest. "I mean, it's strange that Sonia would make a pet of the very creature that killed her."

"Tiny here," Remi said, petting the demonic dog, "was a gift from me so that Sonia could—what is the human expression for this?—get back on the horse again?"

"With a murderous dog?"

At this, Tiny growled.

"Sorry, but you saw the fireflies' dance."

Tiny groaned in resignation.

"First of all," Remi said, "barguests are unfailingly loyal to their master, even if their master is one as vile as Archimago. This barguest —this animal dubbed 'Tiny'—belongs to Sonia, and could no more hurt her than any of us in this room. She needed to understand that if she was to get past the great evil that was visited upon her."

"And that's why Oighrig End had so many uneven, inconsistent wounds. He wasn't killed by one or two people ... he was killed by all of you."

"Aye," said a voice behind me.

Everyone in the room except Ankou bent the knee. I guess when you're the reaper, your bony butt bends for no one. Their heads dropped low as Sonia walked into the room, still holding King Aelfric's hands.

Not being fae, I didn't know where I stood on the *Respect the King* edict, so I just stood there trying not to draw any attention to myself.

"Aye," she repeated, "we all played our roles and took part in ending that murderous bastard. We did so because we wished to share the pleasure of revenge and the guilt of murder. And behold what it has given us: our king, my father."

Sonia held the dark elf's hand tighter as he guided her into the center of the room. There, he let go of her hand and said, "It is so good to see you all again. Especially you, my friend." He walked over to Jack-in-Chains. The giant lowered his head farther as his king drew closer.

The dark elf placed a gentle hand beneath the giant's chin and gently lifted his head. "Come," King Aelfric said, "let me look at you."

Jack's eyes welled with joy for the returned king, and shame for his failure of all those centuries ago.

King Aelfric set his hands on Jack's neck and unclasped the Gleipnir chain. "You've worn this long enough, my friend," the dark elf said, letting go of the chain and locket. The punishing necklace hit the kitchen's linoleum floor with a thud so heavy I was sure he'd just wiped out their entire damage deposit.

Then the Elf King scanned the whole room. "Rise, all of you. Rise."

Ly erg, trow, giant, goblin and abatwas three all rose to their feet and stood before a king who had died centuries ago.

25

I'M NOT GOOD AT BEING GOOD

"*That* was nice," I said, immediately regretting the words as they left my lips. The truth was, it was nice. More than nice, it was beautiful, and my callous comment would probably be considered sarcastic and rude.

But then I remembered I was in a room full of fae. They're a literal bunch, so they all nodded in agreement. All but Sonia, whose human half seemed to register my comment as not quite rude enough to comment on.

"So," I said, silently *phewing* with relief, "what now?"

"Now we wait for the storm to pass so we can leave," Remi said.

I shook my head. "Not going to happen."

King Aelfric looked in my direction, acknowledging me for the first time since entering the room. "First," he said, "I must apologize for my attack. Returning from the dead is ... confusing."

Tell me about it, I thought (in my head).

"And I agree with you: it will not be easy to leave this place. But I suspect our reasons are very different." He gestured for me to speak my mind with a regal wave of his hand.

"Fine," I said. "Because they"—I waved my hands at the motley crew of UnSeelie fae—"killed someone."

"A murderer, a vile human being who—" Sonia started.

"Exactly," I interrupted, "a human being. But even if he wasn't—even if he was the Devil himself—the rules are different now. You can't just kill someone, as deserving as they may be, and go on with your life."

The irony of my words weren't lost on me. I had killed and gotten away with it, and not just as a vampire. Since I had become human, two humans had died because of me. Granted, one of them was an asshole who was trying to mass-sacrifice students in a vain attempt to get the gods back, and the other one was a maniac who drowned himself in a puddle before I could save him, but they died because of me.

I rubbed my temples as if doing so could turn my hypocrisy switch off. "They're going to catch you."

"We have planned for that," Remi said. "This snow has done much to confuse our efforts. Still, it will have to end, and when it does we will dispose of the body where no one will ever find it."

He slapped his hands together three times as if punctuating his words with a *That's that*.

"And what about me?"

"Even after all you've seen—the injustices we've righted, the evil we have removed from this world—you would still turn us over to the authorities?" Redcap said.

"What injustices are you talking about? What happened in the Seelie and UnSeelie Courts was then. Now, in the GoneGod World, all you've done is kill a human professor," I said, considering the last piece of the puzzle. "I don't care if, once upon a time, he was a human sorcerer. I don't care that he's Archimago in the flesh. You killed him."

There was a stunned silence at the name Archimago. "Very good, young lady. I see a bright career for you in law enforcement," Remi said, "Tell me, how did you discover Oighrig End's true identity?"

"It was mostly the questions you asked Professor End during the lecture, but also his name. 'Archimago' is Latin for 'the first and the last,' and Oighrig is Scottish Gaelic for 'new one,' so Oighrig End translates into New One, End ... beginning and end. First and last."

"So if you know who he is and what he's done, why would you tell the authorities?" Remi asked.

"I don't know," I said honestly. "I just know I'm trying to play by human rules now, and what you did was wrong."

"And what would you have us do? Let Oighrig End continue earning accolades and money, honor and respect? After all he's done?"

"You could have turned him in yourself—"

"You talk about the new rules of the GoneGod World like you don't live here," Sonia said. "Do you honestly believe human justice cares about ancient crimes committed against fae? Humans barely acknowledge us except when pushing us to the fringes of their world, or when punishing us."

"You're right," I said. "Others are second-class citizens, and it would be unlikely for the police to have done anything against Oighrig End. Especially given the amnesty program, but that's the whole point of the program: to forgive, to move on. If every Other with a legitimate gripe against another Other or human acted out, this world would never find the peace it deserves."

"And what good would punishing us accomplish?" Krelis asked, pulling Redcap close. I could only guess he was living his personal nightmare of losing him again.

"I don't know," I said, wishing to the damn GoneGods I wasn't the one playing ethical moderator. I'm the last person who should play judge, but I was playing the role because no one else there would. "Because your punishment would send a message that revenge is not OK. Not anymore. Because jailing you would reverberate throughout the Other communities, and if seeing you in chains stops one or two Others from taking justice into their own hands, then that might be worth it."

"He deserved to die," Redcap said.

"Maybe. But how many UnSeelie Court members think the ranks of the Seelie Court deserve death, too? And that's both ways … fae memory is long. How many Seelie Court elves or pixies would happily end the vile lives of goblins, trows and dark elves because of something that happened centuries ago?"

Sonia growled, and for a moment I thought she was going to order my execution. After all, if I died, so did this little moral dilemma. Yay me for standing up for what I believe in in a room of murderers. I'd probably get the Heavenly version of the Girl Scout badge for Death by Righteousness. That was, if Heaven still existed.

But Sonia didn't order my death. Instead she shook her head in frustration and reached for her father's hand. "Do as you must. His death is a crime we would all commit again and again, but know this: you may very well never get a chance to hand us over to the authorities."

I guess ordering my death is back on the table, I thought, and from the way Deirdre came to my side, I guessed it was out loud.

Sonia gave me a disgusted look, as if I had suggested something vile. "No, we would never order the death of an innocent. No matter what stupidity she proposes," she spat out.

Go stupidity, I thought (this time in my head).

King Aelfric nodded in agreement. "You are safe amongst us. Perhaps you are not a friend, but you are also not an enemy. It is this storm that is our true enemy. I have looked into its heart and know that it is impenetrable. I believe it to be the work of magic, but it does not spring forth from the well of fae magic. Nor is it something Archimago, as powerful as he once was, could create. I fear other forces are at play here, magics beyond what we are capable of."

"No, no, no!" Sonia said in frustration. "Your return is my wildest dream come true. But it is also my nightmare, for we are not safe here. My father is not safe here, and if I were to lose him again—"

"It would literally be the worst thing that could happen to you."

She nodded.

"To any of you," I added.

More nods.

I turned to the fae reaper. "Ankou, did you bring him back from the dead?"

The reaper said nothing, and only stared ahead impassively.

"I already told you, young lady: Ankou brought back our king. He must have. Just as he did Sonia all those years ago."

"Exactly. Just like you said: '*all those years ago,*'" I said, keeping my gaze on Ankou. I was looking for a gesture, a facial tic, anything to see if I was right. "Before the gods left he had unlimited power. But he's mortal now, just like you and me." I turned to King Aelfric. "Centuries might have passed since you two last met, but because of your resurrection, it must feel like you saw him only hours ago."

"You speak the truth," King Aelfric said.

"Tell me, do you see any signs of aging on him? Wrinkles, blemishes, a mole, liver spot ... anything?"

"I don't know what you—" King Aelfric started.

"Please, indulge me. Do you see any signs of aging on him at all?"

The dark elf pushed aside his confusion to answer my question. Drawing in close, he examined Ankou closely. The reaper didn't move as Aelfric scoured his face for any signs of aging. After several seconds, the Elf King shook his head. "No. He is as he was that night at the moor."

"Shit," I said. "I know what's happening." And as if the evil that imprisoned us heard my words (she probably did), an explosion thundered through the kitchen with such incredible force that it literally shook the very ground on which we stood.

End of Part 3

145

PART IV

INTERMISSION

Nightmares cannot touch those with nothing to lose. Of course there is always pain, but pain is so boring. There is only so much pleasure one can gain from incessant screaming and wailing.

It is from true suffering my pleasure sprouts. True suffering induced by pure nightmares.

Wealth lost, power diminished, good health gone to seed. A lover sick, a soulmate dying, a child missing, attachments severed. This is the realm of true nightmares.

But these fae are so detached. Their home gone, their spirits broken. They barely hold on to each other. Not one of them has something they hold truly precious. What's more, each would gladly forfeit their lives for something as trivial as revenge.

How can I torment those with nothing to lose? What can I take from those with nothing?

The answer is simple: give them something precious to feel the sting of its loss. Return something they love, only to take it away again.

To lose a precious thing once is pain. But to lose it twice ... that is death. And death is something *I love*.

I have searched their hearts, felt their very essences. They all lost their king, their friend, a man whom they all truly loved, and when they lost him, they also lost themselves.

Let me make them complete. Let me fill them with his presence. Let me make them whole again …

And once they are whole again, well, then I will break them.

26

KINGS, DAY-DREAMS AND NIGHTMARES ALL ROLLED INTO ONE

*T*hunder echoed through the room, metal pots and pans rattling in its wake.

"What the hell is that noise?" Sonia asked, clasping her ears.

Every one of us was rattled. I'd fallen on my butt. Even on the ground, I struggled to find any sense of balance, the floor tossing me around like the uncoordinated kid in a bouncy castle.

The fae, as graceful as they were, didn't fare much better. Jack stomped his massive feet as he tried to find his balance, and each time he brought a foot down he left cracks in the ground. Redcap and Krelis held on to one another, trying to use the other to still themselves, but all they managed to do was engage in an unfortunate game of see-saw.

Deirdre had chosen my tact: fall on your butt, use your arms as a tripod and try not to roll around. *She's not faring much better than me*, I thought, as she was flung from one side of the room to the other.

Remi managed it slightly better than the rest. Well, "better" might be a stretch. He took large, exaggerated steps back and forth like a backup dancer in *West Side Story*. At least he hadn't fallen, and he wasn't destroying the ground to stay on his feet.

The abatwas had all fallen off their counters. Even though it was less than four feet to the ground, for those little guys it must have been like falling off Everest. I was sure they were goners, but they weren't. They shook it off and, helping the one-legged Pop to his feet, scurried under a table where they would be safe from falling pots and pans, or the accidental stomp of one of the larger fae trying to regain their footing.

Even Ankou fell on his butt, but unlike Deirdre and me, he somehow managed to stay relatively still.

Only King Aelfric seemed unaffected by the quake, his feet slightly apart as he helped Sonia stay upright. "Steady," he said. "Feel the movement of the earth. Let the vibrations run through you. Find its rhythm and stand." He let go of his daughter, and Sonia wobbled at first before finally standing up straight.

King Aelfric turned to the rest of us and whispered, "Stand." Even though the word was soft, almost inaudible under the clamoring and clacking of the room, we all heard it and obeyed.

It wasn't a spell. He burned no time, and yet he still inspired us to our feet. Within seconds we were standing on a floor that danced beneath us, and not one of us lost our balance.

We had conquered the quake, and the moment the last of us stood erect, the earth stopped shaking.

Just as I knew it would.

"It's Ester," I said as the world stilled. "She's coming for us. And as strong as you guys might be, she's stronger."

"Ester?" Deirdre asked. "Who's Ester?"

"A better question is, 'What's Ester?' She's a dybbuk demon. She's the stuff nightmares are made of. Literally."

↔

I thought through the sequence of events that had happened. King Aelfric's return, the attack in the boiler room, the stranger with the hockey stick. Being roofied and somehow dragged back into the kitchen ... now that I knew the demon bitch behind it all, things were falling into place.

The guy who hit Aelfric with a hockey stick was Justin ... had to be. Seems that, despite my hopes, he had been possessed by Ester that afternoon in the museum a few weeks back. But the thing about demon possessions—they get you, but they don't get *all* of you. When Justin saved me, it was because the part of him that was still him came out. That, or Ester didn't want to spoil all the fun and kill me too soon. Either way, Justin saved me.

But I couldn't run from the truth. He might have saved me, but neither of us would be in this situation if it wasn't for me exposing him to one of the most evil creatures in creation.

Shit, I thought, *I knew I shouldn't have taken him there. I knew he was too green, and now he's being tormented by a spirit that literally requires an exorcism to get out.*

And given that exorcisms require gods—and those were in short supply—he was fucked. We were fucked, too, because Ester was using his body to carry her evil toward us.

But that was one problem I'd have to deal with later. Now I needed to get my thoughts straight and that meant understanding what happened. The roofied event, with us all being knocked out ... that had to be Ester. She must have seen that her hold on Justin wasn't complete, and not wanting to spoil her fun, decided to knock us out while she tightened her grip on my boyfriend's soul.

As for us all winding up back in the kitchen. The only guy strong enough to do that was King Aelfric. As a trained warrior, he understood that our best chance at survival was unity. Strength in numbers and all that ... so, when the shock of resurrection passed, he must have realized that Jack and I were on the same side, and dragged us back to the kitchen.

That was my theory, at least. Who knows with a psychotic demon like Ester. For all I know, Justin was fully possessed when he saved me from Aelfric, and it was the dark elf's spell that knocked us all out …

Many fae eyes trained on me as they all waited for to tell them what I knew. "I don't have much time to explain," I said, bolting the kitchen door shut. I gestured for Jack-in-Chains to move one of the massive, industrial fridges, which he did as if moving an empty cardboard box. "She's going to attack again, and soon. She's a nightmare spirit, which means she's probably scanning our hearts, trying to figure out the best way to hurt us."

"How do you know this, young lady?" Remi asked.

"I just know," I said as I grabbed a kitchen knife—you know, just in case. There's always a just in case.

"No, young lady. I need more."

"She knows," King Aelfric said, "because the demon and this vampire once hunted together. Is that not true?"

I nodded. No sense in hiding it now, since I doubted we'd survive the night. I had been Ester's partner, but that was a long time ago when we haunted a house together and I was a soulless vampire interested in dinner theatre.

Still, I had tormented enough humans to know how Ester worked. First she'd figure out what you loved the most, and then she'd take it away.

"What is your worst nightmare?" I asked the room. "As a group, what is the one thing that would hurt you the most? Think about it. All nine of you risked so much to avenge your lost king. I know Ester, and I know how she thinks, what she wants. She wants to hurt all of you as badly as she can. And not just hurt you—destroy you in such a way that you would welcome death. That's when she feeds, and that's why I believe it's Ester's magic that brought King Aelfric back from the dead, not Ankou. She did it so she could kill him in some spectacular fashion right in front of you all."

"Never," growled Remi.

Jack-in-Chains smashed his fists together.

And it wasn't just the two warriors. All the fae stood up, ready to fight for their king. Even Deirdre.

Especially Deirdre, who grabbed a stainless steel wok and twirled the giant pan to get a feel for its weight.

So they were going to fight.

Good. And then, remembering how much the dybbuk liked to toy with her prey, I thought: *for Ester.*

27
ONCE MORE ... WITH FEELING!

*T*he impromptu fae army armed themselves with whatever they could find. Redcap grabbed two peelers—nasty fellow—as Krelis armed himself with two heavy rolling pins.

Jack, as if his fists weren't enough, equipped himself with a meat hook from the freezer.

And just when I thought that was it, I saw three corn cob skewers float over the counter past me. The abatwas were dressed for war.

King Aelfric, who knew a battle was coming, picked a long knife for himself and a butcher's cleaver for his daughter. "Redcap and Krelis," he said, "you shall fight by Sonia's side. Jack and Remi, with me.

"Mentan, Coso and Quep,"—three shrieks answered; I guess their names weren't Snap, Crackle and Pop after all—"find a way out of this place. And if that is not possible, then the best vantage point from which we can defend ourselves."

"What about us?" Deirdre said, placing a fist over her heart.

"My changeling friend," he said, "it would be an honor if you and your human friend should fight by our side."

Deirdre gave me a sidelong glance and I nodded. She smiled before pursing her lips once more. "As you command."

Everyone was ready. Everyone but Ankou, who continued his impassive stare.

"You might want to gear up," I said.

"He will not," Sonia answered. "He is a reaper, and must remain impartial to any battles that come."

"I get that he used to play Switzerland, but reaper or not, he's mortal now. We all are. And whatever Ester has planned for us will cut him just as deeply as it will us," I said to the room. I turned to the former agent of death. "You really want to die just standing around? Or do you want to die doing something?"

Ankou's eyes flickered almost imperceptibly, but I was close enough to notice. Then he resumed his thousand-mile stare. "Fine," I said, forcing my knife into his hand. He took it, but only because I wasn't giving him a choice. "Your funeral."

I grabbed another knife. Armed, I turned to my commander in this battle. "Now what, my king?" I said with far less sarcasm than I'd intended.

"You said we are under assault from a nightmare demon?"

I nodded.

"It is my experience that malevolent spirits such as these must be nearby. We must find her and end her."

Again I nodded, seeing where he was going with his plan. But as good as the plan was, I couldn't let it happen. Not the way he intended, at least. "Yes, but there are two problems with your plan." I lifted a finger. "She's possessed my boyfriend—"

"Your betrothed?"

"Fine, my betrothed." I sighed. "So killing him is a no-no. Got it?" I scanned the room. They had all heard me, but with the exception of Deirdre, every single one of them would do what was needed to protect the king. So be it. *I'll do what I must to protect Justin.*

"And second," I said, displaying my other nine fingers, "Ester has unlimited magic—don't ask how, long story—and is seasoned at this kind of game, and is as evil as f—"

But before I could finish, there came a groan I'd heard before— back when I was with Ester.

155

"Great," I said, staring at the barricaded door. "Zombies."

28

DO ZOMBIES DREAM OF UNDEAD SHEEP?

*T*he thing about Ester's zombies: they're not your typical groaning, rotting flesh, humans-ravenous-for-brains type (as if that's not scary enough). Sadly, this dybbuk prefers something with a lot more *ahhh*!

And as the zombie mass banged on the barricaded door, I heard their cries ... cries that made this particular brand of zombie special. It started simply enough, with a voice yelling, "I just wanted a taste of yer twat. Surely that was nae worth mee death."

I recognized the old Inverness accent immediately. Gareth. First guy I made out with—as in ever—on the night a vampire turned me and killed him. *And he wasn't the last guy to die after kissing me*, I sighed.

The next voices were a hodgepodge of memorable victims I'd eaten as a vampire, as well as friends, foes and a smorgasbord of people who died by my hand.

But that was what I heard. From the pained expressions on the others' faces, I knew they'd all gotten their personalized version of hell. And from the way most of them were covering their ears, I knew the cries they heard on the other side of the door were simply awful to them.

Part of me wondered what they were hearing. A bigger part of me hoped I'd never find out.

"You killed me with a kiss," said the voice of a beatnik poet I met in Soho decades ago. He was talented, and after I killed him, I sent his poetry for publication. It was picked up right away, which just made me all the sadder. I had ended a great talent.

"I trusted you," said another.

"I loved you."

"All I wanted was to be with you."

And on and on it went.

"Great," I muttered to myself, "my nightmare is a family reunion of lives I ruined and can never make up for."

"Milady," Deirdre said, her eyes wide as she heard the voices of what she most regretted or feared. But although her eyes glistened with the sheen of trapped tears, she was remarkably well-composed. Whatever she heard she took in stride.

Come to think of it … so did I. I wasn't falling apart or raging with world-crumbling guilt. I heard the groans and anger, the laments and curses of people who had died directly or indirectly by my hands, and it didn't really affect me.

For one thing, I knew Ester's tricks. These weren't the real people I had hurt, just Ester digging around in my brain, trying to find something to break me with. Knowing this took away a lot of the sting.

But it shouldn't have taken away all of it. And given that I was more annoyed than anything, I knew what was happening: my missing piece, my lost soul—without it I could meet the pain and guilt in stride. As if the pain was being dampered by the emotional equivalent of morphine.

My emotions were stunted, dulled, muted. And that pissed me off more than anything else. I *wanted* to feel this. I deserved to feel it. This was an agony I should have bathed in, relished every punishing moment of.

"The voices," I said, "they're tricks. Your worst nightmares are behind that door, but they're not real. Those voices are the lies she's using to try to paralyze you."

Everyone was scared. Remi kept pacing, looking over at Sonia every few seconds. Redcap and Krelis held each other as they backed away from the door. Sonia was probably taking it the hardest, because she stood perfectly still. Fae are creatures who love to dance and sing, and just generally to move. If you ever encounter a fae who is perfectly still, they're either terrified or dead.

Even Ankou wore a frown, which was the most expression I'd seen from the reaper since meeting him.

Redcap and Krelis, who stood hand in hand, cried out, "We had nothing to do with her death! We never let the mortal in. Leave us in peace."

King Aelfric put a hand on each, and their fear immediately left them. "I know that is true," he said, "and those voices are liars." He addressed the room. "The human vampire is right: those voices are tricks by a witch who wishes to use our fear to create chaos. I hear the voices of a hundred human soldiers I once killed. They can no more be outside that door than ogres can fly."

"Your version of flying pigs?" I asked.

The dark elf lifted a curious eyebrow. "Human humor?"

"Very good. Deirdre there could take a few pointers from you, and—"

I was cut off by an all too familiar voice. "Kat, my child, you should never have disobeyed your mother and me by sneaking away that night. If you had only listened, we would all be alive today."

That last voice stung. My father's. Normally hearing him would destroy me, but it didn't. The fact that I could hear his voice and not break down hurt. A lot.

I loved him. Love him. And I killed him.

He deserved my tears.

Growling at the door, I yelled, "We wouldn't be alive today because we would all have died of old age two hundred and fifty years ago!" I punched the fridge blocking the door.

"An old voice?" King Aelfric asked.

"My greatest regret," I replied.

The Elf King turned to the others. "Ignore the voices. They are lies, voices of those long dead."

Sonia, who had been standing still, said, "But you are a voice that was silenced long ago." Then she turned as though she'd heard something unexpected. "You shouldn't be here, and yet you are. Back from the dead. If you can come back"—she turned her head once more, now giving the door her left ear—"maybe others can, too."

I was so focused on Sonia and Aelfric, I didn't notice Jack-in-Chains crying and wringing his hands in the corner. The silent giant had not uttered a word for hundreds of years as part of his penance for failing to guard Heurodis, King Aelfric's wife and Sonia's mother.

I should have known whose voice he'd heard. Whose voice he was resisting.

And Ester was a devious bitch who loved to stack nightmares. Of course, Sonia would be hearing the same voice. That became crystal clear when she pointed at the door. "Jack, this is your chance. Save her. Save my mother."

"No, Jack," King Aelfric cried out with a voice that could have stopped a tsunami.

But Jack was no tsunami. He was a giant who had spent hundreds of years wishing he could undo a single moment.

And once Ester promised him a second chance, I doubted there was a force in this world or any other that could have stopped him.

29

HERE'S WHAT HAPPENS WHEN A VOLCANO MEETS A TORNADO

With a single word—"Heurodis!"—Jack broke his centuries of silence as he ripped through the stainless steel refrigerator, tossing it aside with such force it cracked the kitchen's back wall.

Free of the obstruction, the door burst open and zombies piled in. Not that they stood a chance against Jack's tornado; he ripped through them, smashing zombies against stone walls, stomping them into the linoleum floor, bashing their bodies into each other.

The giant made his way through them, rushing toward Heurodis's voice. But even a giant of unimaginable strength has his limitations, and when he finally made it to Heurodis, what he saw broke him.

There was no beautiful human with long, cascading amber hair. There was no young woman with bright eyes and a wondrous smile. There was just death.

Although Death comes to us all, she approaches each of us differently. In that way, Death is an artist, taking each of us with a unique touch.

Death touched Jack first by showing him Heurodis's putrefied body. Her bones were covered in flesh so dry and taut, the simple act of moving tore her apart. She pointed an accusing finger at Jack, and I can only imagine what she said to him in his final moments. Lies, I'm sure. He was the reason she'd died. His failure had led to Aelfric's death, to Sonia's blinding.

He was too slow.

Too weak.

Too stupid.

That's what I guessed she said to him. In truth, I don't know. While Aelfric and Remi screamed for Jack to return to the room where we battled the zombies, doing everything in our limited power to keep them in the hall, I saw Jack fall to his knees and allow the zombies to swarm over him, ripping flesh and sinew from his body.

With Jack gone, there was no reason to keep the door open. Aelfric and Remi let out a war cry that would have shaken the pillars of Olympus as they pushed back the horde and closed the door.

↔

As soon as the door closed, Remi fell to his knees and began to weep. "Jack," he said, over and over again. "Jack."

Sonia, who understood how she'd been tricked, ran to his side, stumbling toward him in her darkness, guided only by his wails. "It's not your fault, my love. It's not."

Remi grabbed her, hugging her with all his might. "I could have saved him," the ly erg cried out. "I could have saved my brother." His gloveless hands wrapped around her back and I stared at them as the kaleidoscope of blood stains morphed over his hands like water and two more drops of green appeared in the mix.

King Aelfric stood over them, using his immense strength to stop the horde from breaking into the kitchen. From the strain, he wouldn't last much longer, but rather than kicking the ly erg and halfling into action, he let them mourn. A good commander knows that a great loss must be felt, even in the heat of battle.

But only for a moment.

And as that moment passed, he gave silent commands to the rest of us to get into position. Then, looking down at his captain and daughter, he yelled, "To your feet, soldier. Jack's death will be avenged. This I swear. So to your feet, for they will break through, and we must be ready to fight. We must ..."

King Aelfric's voice trailed off as his gaze focused on a point on the floor at the back of the kitchen. I followed his eyeline to see what had caught his attention.

If it wasn't for the corn holders, my human eyes wouldn't have been able to see what he was looking at. But corn holders, small as they are, are quite attention-grabbing when they seem to be floating in the air.

The abatwas. They had found a back door.

30

BACK DOORS AND MAGNET'S HELMET

*K*ing Aelfric leapt into action, commanding Deirdre, Redcap and Krelis to find as much loose and heavy kitchen gear as they could to block the door. They didn't hesitate, gathering everything they could find.

Remi, Sonia and I arrayed as much stuff on the ground as we could to obstruct the zombies' attacks. As intelligent as they sounded, they were still zombies, so cans of food, pots, syrup and oil were great to trip them up. And once a zombie fell, it took them a while to find their feet again.

We were incredibly fast, given how much we were trying to do, but then again, a swarm of the undead is a great motivator (I could just see some jackass putting this in his self-help book). Once our obstacles and traps were in place, we made our way to the back, where Crackle and Pop were smashing through a weak spot in the wall using a meat cleaver and a rolling pin.

These guys were strong.

We finished off their little demolition job with kicks and punches of our own until the hole in the wall was large enough for us to get through one by one.

Sonia was first, followed by Ankou, Remi, Redcap and Krelis (so much for ladies first). I was next, and as Deirdre and King Aelfric made their way through the hole, the zombies were already at our backs.

We all squeezed through by the skin of our teeth (but given how banged up my legs were after crawling over all that loose rubble, the expression should have been "the enamel of our knees").

We found ourselves in one of the basement storage rooms. Cubby hole after cubby hole of student lockers lined the maze. The door to the main hallway was set into one of these walls, not that any of us rushed to find it. We were probably safer in here than out there.

"How do we stop her?" King Aelfric whispered.

"We don't," I said in a low voice. "She's a cursed creature trapped in a box. She's using my boyfriend to carry her around. The first step is to separate them, then bury the box."

"Destroy the box," Remi said, wiping away a tear.

"No!" I whisper-screamed. "That will release her. You think she's bad now? Freed, she'll be unstoppable. Believe me, the only reason we're alive now is because we're fighting the *lite* version of this spirit."

"I can destroy the box," the ly erg said. "I can end her."

King Aelfric put a hand on Remi's chest and pushed him against the wall. "You will do no such thing."

Remi pushed against the dark elf's hand, but couldn't move the king. "I ... I will do what I must."

"I will not lose anyone else this day," King Aelfric hissed, each word laced with venom. "Swear to me."

"But—"

"Swear to me!"

Remi pursed his lips before diverting his gaze and nodding. "I swear."

"What's that all about?" I whispered to Deirdre, figuring she might have some insight into that little exchange.

"He is ly erg, a soldier of the UnSeelie Court. Soldiers have many powers, but perhaps the greatest of them all is that of sacrifice." She gave me a solemn look like that explained everything.

Which, if her goal was to confuse me even more, it did.

. . .

↔

"So separate the boy from the box."

"Well that's a bit cruder than I'd like, but essentially, yes," I said to a confused group (flutter?) of fae. "But we have to find them first and—this is crucial, so listen up—not die in the process."

A zombie groaned to accentuate my point.

"What should we expect out there?"

"I don't know, but when Ester and I would do our little haunted house trick, it was always the same: start with something like zombies or giant spiders or whatever the group most feared, then send them on an impossible quest or mission where we teased out their greatest fears while giving the illusion of the hope that if they succeeded, they'd live. That's how she feeds. Fear. And she used to say that the sweetest fear springs from fading hope."

"And you?" he asked.

"Me? I'm a vegetarian."

The dark elf pursed his lips in a *that's not what I meant and you know it* kind of way.

"Adrenaline. Pump human blood full of it and it tastes like Drambuie. Funny note: put some blood in Drambuie and you get the same results," I said, realizing that my funny note was more of a note that shouldn't have been made.

"Very well," King Aelfric said as he tried to work through a problem with no solution. "How about hiding from her?"

"You can't. Not unless you can suppress every ounce of fear you now feel. I don't know about you, but I'm terrified. And from the looks of you,"—I stared at each of them—"you all looked scared. Even Mr. Reaper here."

Ankou nodded, and everyone in the darkened room gasped. Never before had a fae reaper done anything but watch. To nod, to acknowledge something said or felt, was unheard of in the fae world.

"We all have fears. Mine are the voices of the lives I took as a vampire. The voices I heard were them coming back from the dead to torment me. King Aelfric already told us he heard Orfeo's soldiers, and we know who Jack and Sonia heard … Heurodis. You all heard someone, and I can see how shaken up you are. Tell me, is that a fear you can put away? Because that's what you need to do if you want to hide from the dybbuk.

"In other words," I said, turning to Aelfric, "unless you have a fear switch for each of us, or a fear cloaking device, we're doomed."

King Aelfric smiled. "Fear cannot be dismissed, but it can be masked."

31

WE'RE OFF TO SEE THE WIZARD ...
AHH, I MEAN WITCH

"*I* will not let you go without me," Sonia said, and something iridescent glimmered in her grasp. I looked more closely, and realized it was the abatwas' thistle blade. "Wherever you go, I go."

"But Sonia, you are being unreasonable," Remi said. "The plan is a simple one: the warriors hunt this witch down as the rest of you hide in—"

"Fear?"

"As a distraction. We are going to fight, and you are—"

"Blind?"

Remi looked at King Aelfric for support, but in response, the dark elf lifted his hands in surrender. "I have long learned only to fight battles I have a chance at winning. She is as stubborn as her mother, and this is one battle I cannot win."

Remi groaned in frustration and turned to Sonia. "Please, my love, you are the only one who can sing with enough fear to draw them away."

"And I am blind," Sonia spat. "Do not lie to me. Not when death is so close."

"Very well, my love," Remi said, taking her hands in his. "I shan't, then. You are blind, but that is not why I do not wish you to join us.

You are my heart, my everything. I cannot fight what nightmares may come if I am always looking over my shoulder to see that you are unharmed."

"And I cannot sit here praying to gods that are no longer here that you will return. Nor can I do nothing while my father faces real death —again."

"Sonia, my love, I swear your father will return to you."

"And you? Do you swear that you will return to me as well?"

Remi said nothing.

"No, you don't," Sonia said, reading his silence for what it was. The fae took oaths and promises very seriously. If the ly erg soldier swore his return, then it meant he would have to hold himself back in battle. He'd have to take the safest route and avoid battles that weren't a guaranteed success.

In other words, swearing he'd return would hobble him. And Remi was too experienced a warrior to do that. He knew what lay before us and he wasn't about to make a promise he wasn't one hundred percent sure he could keep.

"My love," he said, "when we came up with this plan to kill Archimago and avenge your father, we swore that we would do whatever it took. We succeeded in our plan, but because of this vampire—"

"Human," I interjected.

"—*human* vampire, a malevolent spirit threatens us with death. I made an oath a long, long time ago to protect you. We all did, swearing it on your father's name. Please, let me fulfill my oath. Stay here, sing your song and draw them to you."

Sonia's unseeing eyes dripped with tears. "But should you die ..."

"Then you will go on. I would die a thousand times if it meant your survival, gladly go into the endless darkness if it granted you one more day. If I die, you live. But I do not wish to die. I wish to spend a million breaths by your side. I swear this: I will do whatever I can to return, but I do not swear to do so if it means there is a chance you will be harmed. Agreed?"

Remi clasped Sonia's unblemished hands in his own blood-stained ones. "That has to be enough," he said.

Sonia shook her head before nodding. "Everything you can."

"Everything I can," he repeated.

"Very well," she said, "then I will stay here."

"And sing?"

"And sing," she said, using the sound of his last words to find his lips and draw them to her own.

↔

"Remember," King Aelfric said, kissing his daughter's forehead, "you have to express enough fear that the hag cannot help but pursue you. That will clear our way."

"You and my betrothed are leaving to face an unimaginable evil. Do not worry, Father, I have plenty of fear within me."

"You are so much like your mother," he said.

We cracked the lock on the door and walked into the hall. Behind us, we heard the fae barricading the door with anything they could find. With them as safe as our circumstances would allow, I led the way as we started down the—thankfully empty—hall.

"You have a way with her," King Aelfric said.

Remi nodded, allowing a smile to brighten his face. "I love her. Why did you hide her? If she had remained in the castle, I would have protected her with—"

"I couldn't trust anyone with her. King Orfeo entered our kingdom not by Archimago's magic, but through one of our own."

I stopped and turned. "What do you mean it wasn't Archimago?"

"I mean that one of us betrayed me to the human king. One who did not approve of my human wife."

"Redcap?" Remi said, his eyes flashing with a mixture of fear and anger.

"Calm yourself, soldier," Aelfric said. "I do not know who. My spies only confirmed that one amongst our ranks did so. But that is something we will deal with later ... should we live."

"Yeah," I said. "You killed a human who had nothing to do with your whole revenge plot. Do you still object to me turning you in?"

Remi pursed his lips and said nothing.

"Let us live this night, and then let your conscience guide you," King Aelfric said. "Where is the hag hidden?"

"I don't know for sure," I said. "I don't think she's changed all that much over the centuries, and when we used to work together, she always liked a room with a view."

32

ESTER AND THE LOOKING MIRROR

Sonia's song was perfect, at least for us. Anyone who had to sit through it would probably be reduced to a bubbling mess of fear, but as a distraction for us to move about unnoticed … well, I guess one lady's 'perfect' is another's nightmare (specifically, a goblin, trow, reaper and abatwa's nightmare).

As for our own fear, we were all thinking happy thoughts. I was replaying *Legally Blonde* in my head for the umpteenth time. I suspected that Remi and Aelfric both thought about the same person when masking their fears: Sonia. And as for Deirdre …

"Penny for your thoughts," I whispered to the changeling as we made our way to the upper floors of the building and the rooms with the best views.

Deirdre held out her hand.

"What do you need?"

"A penny," she said, "for my thoughts." She gave me a solemn look as her hand remained outstretched, waiting for a penny.

Since pennies were out of circulation, I couldn't give her one even if I wanted to. Besides, I had left my purse behind. I didn't have any money on me at all. "I'm sorry," I said, "I'm fresh out."

We were in A-House now, and there were only two apartments here. Remi took the left and Aelfric the right.

She pulled her fingers into a fist and gave me a disappointed look. "Did I do that wrong?"

Deirdre and I waited on the landing, ready. We had already checked the other apartments and this was the last place they could be. The two fae warriors were going to scout the apartments—hopefully unde-tected—and return with a lay of the land. That was the plan, at least.

"What?" I asked, regretting asking her anything in the first place.

"My joke. I know you weren't being literal in offering me a penny. I thought by pretending to take your words at face value, I'd be achieving what you humans refer to as humor."

I chuckled. "Not bad. Not bad at all."

Deirdre nodded. "You appreciate my attempt, but not my execu-tion. Understood." She blinked rapidly several times, as if the action would somehow help her file the information away. "I assume your question refers to what I'm thinking about to keep my fears at bay."

"Yes," I said.

"Ryan Reynolds, and how one day we'll be united. Ester tried to strike me down with Ryan's angelic voice crying out that we will never be together. But a love like ours is so complete that I dismissed her evil glamor for what it was … a lie."

"Ahh, I see," I said. I did, too: Deirdre had several of the actor's posters on her walls because she was in love. And I don't mean a child's infatuation. Fae love is forever, and when they give you their hearts, they mean it. Deirdre loved Ryan Reynolds, and it didn't matter to the changeling that all she knew of him were his movies and pictures she'd seen online or on posters.

Fae love, the strongest bond in the known universe. With Remi and Aelfric returned, I saw that bond tethering them to Sonia, she the link now irrevocably connecting these two fae.

"She's not in any of the rooms," Aelfric said.

"I thought you said she liked a room with a view," Remi spat without any attempt at hiding his anger.

"That's what she liked back then," I growled back. "I mean, she's a spirit trapped in a box the size of a Rubik's Cube. Wouldn't you want a room with a view if you were cooped up in something like that?"

"Aye, but with all this snow there is no room here with any view of worth," Aelfric said.

"True," I said, "but you take what you can get, after all—"

"Milady," Deirdre interrupted in a way very unlike her, "when did you say you last frolicked with the spirit?"

"I'd hardly call it 'frolicking.'"

"You mentioned that you two played together ... in an evil way."

"I did, didn't I?" I was starting to hate Deirdre's literal interpretations. Who was I kidding? I *always* hated Deirdre's literal interpretations. "A century ago, at least."

"And has she ahh ... played with anyone else?"

"To the best of my knowledge, no. When we parted ways, she bounced around from owner to owner for a while before eventually winding up in a museum."

"Then I think I know where she is," Deirdre said.

↔

Deirdre led us to the common room with the big screen T.V. "What amazed me most about the GoneGod World was the humans' magic window. The one that let you see the world without actually moving," she said.

Of course, I thought, *a room with a view.*

As we drew closer to the room, we could hear music blaring as an ominous voice said, "Space: the final frontier. These are the voyages of the starship *Enterprise*. Its continuing mission: to ..."

"Who is that?" King Aelfric said.

"Patrick Stewart. Well, Captain Picard. Actually, Patrick Stewart playing Captain Picard," I said, and now it was the fae's turn to give me a confused look.

Payback's sweet, I thought as I placed a finger over my lips. "She's in there."

Remi and Aelfric both pulled out their improvised kitchen weapons and said, "We'll flank her from the left and right. You two attack head on. Let's end this curse once and for all."

"And no hurting Justin."

"Who?"

"The human holding the box. The mission is to get the box away from him and carry it as far from this place as possible."

Remi nodded. "I know exactly where to take it."

33
I'M AN IDIOT ... SERIOUSLY, I AM

*T*he plan was simple enough, and given the kind of muscle we had between a dark elf, a ly erg, a changeling and *moi* (I might be small, but I'm mighty!), it should have been an easy win. Attack, get the box, make a run for it.

Simple-*calafragalisticexpialidocious*. It was a plan with a lot of potential, a lot of hope. And given that Justin stood inches away from the T.V., his back facing the open door, we should have been a shoo-in.

I'm an idiot, I thought way too late to abort. Because just as the four of us were about to coordinate our strikes, Justin's neck snapped around *Exorcist* style, his eyes neon orange. A blinding energy burst out of his body.

The blinding light engulfed us, pushing us together into one ball before Justin walked backward, pushing us out the door we'd entered by. Once we were outside, the strange energy let us go.

Remi and Aelfric landed on their feet, lunging at my poor, possessed boyfriend.

"No!" I cried out, but it was too late. They both crashed into an invisible wall filling the doorway.

"Shield's up," a voice that was both Ester and Justin said, before casually walking back to the T.V.

"An impossible mission with a lot of hope—just to ripen us up," I said, helping Remi to his feet. "That's the kind of fear she likes to feed on."

"Fear after hope is dessert, dearie," Ester and Justin's dual voice said. "But despair after *all is lost* … that is the main course."

Justin cradled Ester's box in his hands as he took a step to the side, showing us the T.V. screen. It no longer played *Star Trek*. Instead, it showed the storage room we had left the others behind in. On the screen, we watched as zombie after zombie crawled into the room from the hole we had made, the barricade long gone.

That might have been all right, except that the hole was getting larger as dead hands dug at the sides to widen it. In a few minutes, it would be large enough for them to walk through.

Not that they were waiting until then. Two zombies crawled through and their heads were promptly bashed by Krelis's rolling pins. But a third managed to get through when the two zombie bodies were dragged from the hole, and two more clambered through. The zombie that got through was dispatched by Ankou, who used the kitchen knife I gave him to gut the undead creature from Adam's apple to navel.

Way to go, Mr. I-Only-Observe!

Even the abatwas were doing their part by stuffing the hole with items from the storage room, slowing the zombies' progress.

And all the while, Sonia drew them in with her song. Her face was strained, but I saw a resolve there I've seen on the faces of mothers guarding their young, of soldiers fighting to save their squad, of truly selfless beings protecting their loved ones.

She would sing until her family was safe, or she was dead. Whichever came first.

"No, no!" Remi said, banging his fists against the unseen window.

I turned to Deirdre and yelled, "Go—help them!"

Deirdre dashed away. Remi started to follow her when Aelfric's regal voice cried out, "Stop!"

177

"I have to save her. I have to—"

"Stand here with us and fight."

Remi turned to the door, his tainted fists balled up in frustration.

"Are you sure you should be listening to your once king, ly erg?" the dual voice said. The screen's focus shifted to Sonia as a zombie reached out for her. Ankou pulled the zombie back, but unless we stopped Ester soon, they were doomed. "Run. If you can't save them all, maybe you can save her."

The ly erg shook his head. "I stand with my king."

"Interesting," they said. "Then perhaps we should ask a more pertinent question: does the king wish for you to stand with him?"

"On my honor," Aelfric said, placing a fist over his chest.

"On your honor," the voices cackled. Justin lifted a hand and the T.V. displayed not a storage room filled with zombies, but a brook in the middle of a field.

There Remi stood, his hands relatively clean compared to what they were now. He placed a hand with only a bit of green in the water and dragged his fingers against the stream.

It was daytime where Remi stood, but the line he drew revealed a world sunk into night. And through that portal stepped a lone man.

Orfeo.

↔

"It was you?" Aelfric said, his voice no longer imbued with regal authority; he sounded like he was begging for his murderer to stop. "You? You are the reason Heurodis was killed? The reason my Sonia is blind?"

"Lies!" Remi cried out.

"No lies," the dual voice said. "I never lie. Ask Katrina—she knows."

I nodded, my gaze passing from Aelfric to Remi. Before me stood two seasoned warriors on the brink of finding some corner to curl up in and die. I thought about lying to them, using that lie to patch them up enough to stay in the fight.

But it was no good—I could see Aelfric processing everything that had happened before and after his wife's death. He already knew the truth, though his heart had yet to accept it. Telling him the truth would be the fastest way for that to happen. And once he accepted it, maybe, just maybe he'd get back into the fight.

"Part of the reason Ester's so good is because she only speaks the truth. A truth that distorts and manipulates, but always the truth."

"No. The human vampire lies, too." But Remi's panicked voice betrayed him.

"Ester always tells the truth, but that's not the only way to see it. Your hands—I saw them become more deeply tainted with green blood after Jack died. That can only happen if you're responsible for his death, and since you are the reason Heurodis died, you are the reason for his guilt and ultimately for him charging through a horde of zombies. His blood is on your hands."

Remi shook his head violently. "No, it's not true. It's not—"

"The truth!" Aelfric cried out, his voice so powerful I felt like I should confess everything I'd ever done in my life—like, ever. And I wasn't the one on trial.

Remi stopped his head shaking, stopped his prattling. Stopped moving altogether. He stared ahead, acceptance painted not only on his face, but on his whole being.

He fell to his knees and said in a distant, sorrowful voice, "A soldier without war is nothing. When I let Orfeo into our realm, I thought one of our guards would capture him before he reached our walls. I believed that seeing a human in our lands would be enough to warrant war. I didn't know he would slip past the guards, that he would make it to Heurodis's chamber and kill her. I didn't know then that my brother, Jack, would take it so hard. He wore that chain for over a thousand years, didn't speak a word to anyone for over a thousand years. All because of what I'd done. So yes, his blood is on my hands." He held out his left palm, the one stained with new green blood.

"And the barguests that blinded Sonia? Was that part of you not wanting to hurt her?" I said.

Remi closed his eyes, the weight of his words forcing out tears he could no longer hold back. "I was trying to force war. If the death of your wife wouldn't spur you to action, then perhaps the death of your daughter would."

His calm, detached voice suddenly became imbued with feeling as he thought of Sonia. He opened his eyes and looked at me with eyes that begged me to hear him—were desperate that I hear him. "At that moment, I only saw her as a half-breed child who distracted our king from what must be done. But that was then, before I knew her. Before I saw who she really was and fell in love with her. That is why I did all this. I hunted down Archimago, created this scenario, all to offer my beloved Sonia a chance for closure.

"And look. In doing so, I have given her something much more: our king, her father. You have returned."

"It's not me you have to convince," I said.

Turning to King Aelfric, Remi fell to his knees. "I never wanted to hurt you or Sonia. I just wanted you to open your eyes. Force you to see what a life hidden in the UnSeelie Court was costing us."

"And so you chose for us to pay another price altogether?" the Elf King asked.

"Aye," Remi said, lowering his head. He looked into the room; the T.V. had returned to a view of the storage room. Several zombies were inside now, but so was Deirdre. Thank the GoneGods for small miracles.

"King Aelfric," Remi said, his voice calm as he stared at the scene, "I know I am undeserving, but will you allow me one last chance to serve you?"

The dark elf said nothing.

"One last chance to undo some of the wrong I've done." Remi bent deeper, exposing the back of his neck. Amongst the UnSeelie, this was a request for a dagger to be thrust into the neck.

"What will you have me do?" the Elf King asked, pulling the kitchen knife from his belt.

"What you must. End me now, or free me from my promise to you."

King Aelfric looked up, pain dancing across his lips. The choice Remi offered him was simple: kill him, or allow him to be killed. It is not easy for a fae to release someone from an oath. To do so means to forgive them everything they have done.

That meant forgiving Remi for the death of his wife, the blinding of his child, and an act so heinous that it led to his suicide. That was a lot for the Elf King to forgive. I mean, could you forgive someone who took away everything you ever loved?

The dark elf's hand trembled as he wrestled with the choice before him. "My most trusted soldier, my friend. If Death comes to you this day, then let him embrace you as who you were to me—who I would like to remember you as." King Aelfric dropped the knife and placed his empty palm on Remi's head. "Rise."

Remi stared up at his once-upon-a-time king, his hands before him. I noticed the new green stain—Jack's blood—wash off his hands. So too did the red stain, Heurodis's blood. Both were gone.

I guess when an Elf King forgives you, he really forgives you.

"Thank you," Remi whispered, and with the resolve of a true soldier who knows everything is lost, he stood. The ly erg spoke, but not to his king this time. He spoke to me. "You say that this evil spirit is trapped within that plain wooden box."

I nodded. And just in case he got any bright ideas, I added, "She's contained there. Breaking the box will release the evil spirit, and I don't know any way to kill it."

"You may not, but I do," Remi said. "For you, for my friends, for Sonia and for my king."

He lifted two fingers to the center of his forehead as he concentrated. He started to hum, and with that hum I felt a surge of emotions that created a cloud within me. Anger and despair, but also hope and the courage to finally do the right thing.

Remi placed the two fingers on Ester's shield and pushed. As he did so, his hum grew into a rage-filled scream that burst the shield into a million fractals of crackling energy.

With no shield to stop him, the ly erg leapt forward with impossible speed. Impossible for any being not burning time, and as he moved forward, I saw his hair greying.

He wasn't just burning some of his time—he was burning all of it.

Grabbing the box from Justin, he cracked it open like an egg. As Ester's spirit flew out of the cursed item, he sucked in her essence, trapping her within himself.

Finally free, Justin fell to his knees as consciousness left him. I rushed over, pulling his limp body away from Remi and Ester as they continued their macabre dance.

The struggle between the two determined souls only took a handful of seconds. Hardly enough time to pay proper respect to the magnanimous event taking place. Ester struggled to break free, and Remi continued to suffocate her with his very being.

With a crackle that would have sent Zeus himself running in fear, it was over.

Remi's body stood hunched over as though in prayer, aged beyond recognition. But there was no movement, no rise and fall of breath. No sign of life.

"What ... what did he do?"

King Aelfric answered. "A ly erg is granted a single wish that may be asked at the moment of death. Remi's must have been for the power to contain the hag." The king walked over to Remi's unmoving body and placed a gentle hand on his back. "The price of that wish was a soldier's sacrifice. Death."

Remember how every fae has a unique "thing"? Seems that a ly erg's thing is the ability to go out with a bang.

I guess some wishes are still granted in this GoneGod World, I thought as I stared at the fallen ly erg's unmoving body.

34
GOODBYES AND GOODBYES

*A*s soon as Remi consumed Ester, the zombie horde melted away like a scene out of *The Wizard of Oz*. And the mindless dead weren't the only thing that stopped: the snow stopped falling, too. Ester's curse was lifted.

Not that anyone felt joy about being freed. Ester might have been gone, but what she had done wasn't about to melt away. Jack-in-Chains and Remi were gone, and there was no magic in this world to bring them back.

Justin came out of his possession as though waking from a coma. I got down on the floor and held him tight as he slowly started to comprehend what had happened. He might have had a demon pulling his strings like some shadow puppet, but it was his body that did everything, his eyes that saw everything, and his being that would, in time, remember everything.

"I ... I'm so sorry," he eventually said.

"Shush," I whispered in his ear. "I'm just happy you're safe." But that happiness quickly became pain as I thought about what I'd have to do to make sure Justin stayed safe.

Aelfric was already gone, and I knew exactly where he'd gone: to

Sonia, to make sure she was all right. So Justin and I stayed where we were and waited for the others to come.

They did. First Deirdre rushed in with the look a mother wears when she's found her lost child and sees she's not hurt. Sonia was next. The blind halfling, led by her barguest Tiny, rushed to Remi's side, where she held his dead body and cried.

King Aelfric, Redcap, Krelis and Snap, Crackle and Pop (I know those weren't their names, but I couldn't remember what Aelfric called them, and besides … come on, if the cereal tastes good, eat it!) and finally Ankou.

The fae reaper looked worse for wear, like he'd ridden Space Mountain when he was expecting the Epcot Center. His eyes were wide, his expression shell-shocked. And I think I knew why: he'd finally understood he was mortal. After an eternity of being immortal *and* a reaper, I'm guessing you never really think about your own death. Now that the gods are gone and everyone is mortal, well, it takes some Others longer than others for the mortality to sink in.

I knew exactly what he was going through.

But as traumatic as that realization was, Ankou was a professional. He made his way to Remi and put his hand on the ly erg's head before chanting the warrior's funeral rites.

I looked at Aelfric, expecting the dark elf to stop the reaper, tell them all of Remi's betrayal and how the ly erg didn't deserve an honorable send-off. But Aelfric did none of that. He just held his head low and respectfully waited for Ankou to finish.

I saw then why they loved him so much.

Next we made our way to Jack, whose body had been shorn to ribbons of flesh hanging loose over his massive frame. Again Ankou preformed the warrior's rite, while Redcap and Krelis, burning some time, repaired his body for send-off.

With that done, it was time for me to assume my role of Negative Nancy. "We've got three dead bodies. This place is torn up. The police aren't going to accept justified murder, and the school isn't going to give you back your deposit."

Everyone heard me, but no one spoke for a long moment until

Snap, Crackle and Pop started their shrieking speech. I didn't understand what they said, but—and I wish this was a joke, but I can't make this up—they pulled out a shovel, pickaxe and hard helmets from only the GoneGods know where and rushed off.

"Taken care of," King Aelfric said.

"And the bodies?" I asked.

Redcap stepped forward, holding his orange wig in hand. "We have that taken care of, too."

↔

We waited until night before placing the bodies in an old-school bus that Redcap owned. I don't know what was more surprising: that Redcap had a bus, or that someone gave him a friggin' license to drive it. Either way, we got the bodies inside, careful to respect them as best we could given our suboptimal funeral car.

Redcap drove up onto Pine, then up a winding road that cut through Mont-Royal and toward Beaver Lake, where he backed the bus as close to the water as he could.

Justin and I held back as the fae approached the water, their hands outstretched as they hummed. A kelpie sprang from the lake, its massive, horselike head dripping as it rose. I guessed the rumors about the Loch Ness Monster living in Beaver Lake weren't an exaggeration after all.

It looked at the fae before fixating on King Aelfric and snorting so loudly they were all showered with lake water. Then it lurched forward, rubbing its snout on the dark elf's chest.

"Yes, yes," King Aelfric said, "I missed you, too. But Earro'on, as joyous as it is to see you, we come to ask you to perform a solemn task once more." Aelfric stood aside and gestured at the bus, its rear door open to reveal the fallen fae inside.

Earro'on snorted once more before nodding.

What happened next was something that can only occur when the bizarre meets the beautiful. They performed final rites and presented the bodies to the kelpie, who dragged them deep into the lake.

First was Archimago. I watched as the fae paid their respects to someone they considered an enemy of the state. Regardless of how they felt about him, they spoke his deeds, evil and good. It seemed Archimago had gone a long way to atonement when he became Oighrig End, the revisionist historian who spoke the Others' truth.

But here he was ... dead for a crime he did not commit. And what's more, his body would never be found, his killers would never be brought to justice. Part of me wanted to scream in anger and fury at the injustice. But part of me accepted this fate. As the Archimago, he had done great evil and, because of who he was and not what he was trying to become, he paid the ultimate price.

As the two parts of my sense of right and wrong wrestled, I thought about myself. My own past ... everything vile and horrible that I'd done as a vampire, and the little good I'd done as a human. I suspect the day I die will be in the service of me trying to undo some of that wrong. And as fair or unfair as my death may be, I will accept it, for it will be retribution for all the evil I've committed. My only hope is that day comes far enough in the future that I will have gone a long way in unburdering my soul.

Next was Jack. King Aelfric used his incredible strength to carry the giant to the shoreline. He carefully laid the giant down and started to tell stories about this incredible creature. And in every word, King Aelfric showed nothing but admiration for the giant, never blaming him for the death of his wife. There was no doubt that as far as the Elf King was concerned, Jack-in-Chains was a good and honorable man.

Finally it was time to lay Remi to rest. Sonia stepped forward and set her hand on his, lifting it to her mouth. She kissed his knuckles while tears ran from her brilliant eyes. Despite all he did, she still loved him, just as she had always truly loved him.

As for King Aelfric, this was when I expected him to finally condemn the fallen ly erg. But he didn't; he only spoke the truth.

The story Aelfric told wasn't one of condemnation or anger. It was simply filled with sadness. In the end, it was Aelfric who gave Remi's body to the kelpie. And as the king delivered the ly erg to his final resting place, I saw that Remi's hands were no longer tainted with blood as they should have been.

His hands were clean.

Earro'on accepted the three dead and took them with him as the kelpie submerged into the water.

I watched the fae as this happened and what I saw in the halfling, trow and goblin, reaper and abatwas were seven creatures who, once upon a time, had been hurt so badly their lives were all but forfeit. And because the fates, universe or whatever still guides the events of our lives that cannot be dismissed as random—gods or no gods—they were made whole again.

They had a chance to be a family again.

A chance to be happy again.

↔

After the fae funeral, I bid the old, newly reunited family farewell. I wouldn't call the police. After all, who would believe me? There were no bodies to speak of, and I doubted they'd fish the lake for an elephant-sized lake monster with the head of a horse.

As for my guilt about Archimago, he had done evil—lots of it. A part of me thought that while the gods might be gone, karma wasn't. He paid for his crimes with his life. And it was his death that had helped to bring a family together and heal many wounds of the past. Whether that was right or not, I wasn't sure. All I did know was the scales were a little more balanced because of what had happened.

Everyone started to go on their way. Everyone but Ankou. The fae reaper approached me, and in his usual creepy way, stared at me until Justin and Deirdre, who were standing next to me, got the hint and left my side.

Then he did something that Deirdre would not believe when I told her about it later, no matter how many times I said "I swear" or crossed my heart, or how many oaths I made.

Ankou spoke.

↔

"Thank you for your aid back there," the reaper said, his voice surprisingly normal sounding. I don't know what I expected—Vincent Price, maybe? "And for your words. You are right: the old world is gone. So too are the old ways. *My* old ways. My impassive ways." The reaper sighed as if taking a breath for the first time. "And to that end, I wish to repay you with a warning. Of all the substances in this world or any other, the human soul is of the highest value."

I shook my head. "Here we go with the soul business again. My soul isn't missing, because you can't lose your soul. It's a part of you, not something that can be ripped away."

In response, the reaper stood perfectly still, his expression impassive. *So much for taking a more active role in things*, I thought.

Ankou's lips curled as he nodded. "Again, you are correct. It seems I have fallen into old habits, so let me explain further. The human soul is something that cannot be mined, cannot be forged or counterfeited. Only Life births a soul, and only Death frees it." The reaper paused. "Do you know why the gods demanded worship from their human creations?"

"I don't know. Ego?"

Ankou shook his head.

There had been a theory floating around that the gods actually got their power from human worship. The more they were worshipped, the more powerful they became. "Power," I said.

Much to my surprise, Ankou shook his head again.

"Then tell me." I was getting frustrated.

"Souls were what allowed the celestial worlds to ..." he paused, searching for the word, "... be. When the gods left, they closed their heavens and hells not by will or power or magic, but by emptying their domains of human souls. The heavens and hells are not just closed. They are also empty. But should one single human soul find its way into one of the domains, well, that can change everything."

I thought about that for a moment as the gravity of what he'd just said dawned on me. "You mean a single human soul can reopen Heaven? Or Hell, or Elysium or Tartarus?"

The reaper nodded.

"Then why not stand over a dying person's bed and capture the soul as it leaves the body?"

"Ahh, if only it were so simple," he said. "Make no mistake, there are Others of great power trying to accomplish that very deed, but to capture a human soul is akin to trapping the wind. Not so easy." He lifted a bony, gray finger and touched my forehead. "As a way of thanking you for your aid on this day, I offer you a warning. You live without your soul. There will be those who will seek to exploit this anomaly, and therefore, you."

And as if those cryptic words were payment enough for helping to protect his king and righting an ancient wrong, he folded his arms and walked past me without so much as a second glance.

↔

"So," Justin said, "that was crazy."

Speaking of karma, I thought.

"Huh?" Justin said.

"Never mind," I said, waving away my out loud thoughts. This conversation was going to be hard enough without the wrong thoughts being aired. "Justin, we need to talk."

"We do," Justin said, reaching for my hand as we walked. I pulled mine away. He didn't reach for me again. "I just wanted to say thank you. For saving me."

"Is that what I did? Aren't I the one who endangered you in the first place?"

"The only danger I'm in is explaining to my parents why I didn't come home for Christmas … or call them. That's going to be a doozy …" he trailed off, probably thinking about what he was going to tell them.

But that was *his* problem. My problem was *him*. "Justin, if it wasn't for me you would never have been anywhere near that dybbuk. You would never have been possessed."

"True, but I don't see it that way," Justin said. "I … I was the stupid one. I said something when you told me a dozen times to keep my mouth shut. I didn't, so it's on me."

I stopped walking. "No, Justin, it's on me. I'm the three-hundred-year-old in this relationship. I'm the one who should have known better."

"What? Am I a kid who needs his—"

"Yes, you are. You're nineteen. Nineteen. You should be going to bars and studying and getting stoned with your buddies. You should be doing things kids do. And what you *shouldn't* be doing is following around an *ex*-vampire as she tries to make up for all the killing she's done."

"You were a vampire back then, Kat. It's not—"

"No, Justin, you don't understand. I remember every single life I took. I remember how they looked, how scared they were, how they tasted … every detail. I know that the demon in me demanded human blood, but I wasn't completely *not* me. I was still there. I could have fought harder, like my father did."

"He killed himself the day he was turned."

I widened my eyes and nodded. "I should have, too. How many family tree branches were severed by me? How many?"

Justin didn't answer, looking away.

"You don't know. Well, neither do I. All I know is that I'm going to keep getting myself in dangerous situations as I try to make up for some of that. Again and again, until the day I die. I will do that with the hope that when I go, my soul is just that little bit lighter."

Soul, I thought, *as if I have one.*

"And I'll help you every step of the way."

"Good," I said. "You can help me by leaving me alone. I can't keep doing what I'm doing if every step I take puts you in danger."

"Kat, I don't mind the danger. I just want to be with—"

"Then you're an idiot. Just like anyone else who willingly puts themselves in danger. In the four months you've known me, you've been beat up, kidnapped and possessed by a demon. Do you really think you're strong enough or smart enough to survive me much longer?"

He started to answer, and I put a hand up to stop him. "Let me answer for you. You're not."

He winced, his eyes closing as he tried to shut away the pain.

Good, I thought. *Time to go in for the kill just like I've done so many times before.*

"Maybe if you were strong enough we could be together, but you're not. You've proven that over and over. This is it. We're done, Justin. We're done."

I walked away from him, leaving behind the nineteen-year-old kid who was too stunned to follow. As soon as I was sure I was far enough away that he couldn't hear me or catch up, I broke down in tears.

35
AND BEFORE YOU KNOW IT ...
YOU'RE IN JAPAN

"Happy New Year, Kat," Dr. Tellier said, wearing that same stupid smile he always does. "Well, it's not the new year quite yet, but given we're a few days away and I'll probably not see you again between now and then, I thought I'd get a jump start on the whole thing."

I ignored him and sat down in a huff. He was far too cheerful given the mood I was in.

"From your demeanor, I'm guessing it's the 'happy' part that's in question."

"It's not in question, Dr. Tellier. 'Happy,' 'joy,' 'merry,' and just about any other synonym you can think of didn't find its way to me. Now, if you want to talk antonyms ..."

"Hah. At least you've kept your sense of humor."

"Barely," I said.

"Want to talk about it?"

"No."

"OK, let me rephrase my question: should we talk about it?"

"I broke up with my boyfriend." My eyes widened as I tried to recall those words. The last thing I wanted to talk about was Justin.

"You did? Why?"

Too late. I sighed. "I still love him, but I'm no good for him."

"As in not good enough for him?"

I mean, come on, I thought, *I'm cute as a button, smart, strong ... rich.* Not that I said any of that (thankfully). Instead I let my *you're smarter than that* look answer the question for me.

"So then what do you mean by 'no good for him'?"

"I mean bad things happen to people I love. So I figured I'd try not loving for a bit."

"I see. And these bad things ... what do you mean by that?"

I thought about telling him who I was, and what had happened to me during my one semester at McGill. The fights, the funerals, the hate. And most recently I had walked away from Oighrig End's death. I had claimed I would hold the fae to task, but in the end I hadn't sought any justice for a murdered professor. That one weighed pretty heavily, too.

Instead of telling him all that, I chickened out and did what I always seem to do when the conversation gets hard: I changed the subject and made a joke. "The last time we spoke you said there are no cookie-cutter solutions, right? I can't go to the Walmart for the Insane and pick something off the shelf?"

"If you could, I'd be out of a job," he chuckled.

"And that would be a bad thing?"

The counselor didn't do the typical joke, or dismiss what I thought was a throwaway comment. Instead, he paused and thought about it. I mean, he actually thought about it. After a long moment of consideration, he said, "Yes, that would be a bad thing. Not the part about mental struggles disappearing—that is harsh, and causes a lot of pain for many people. If I could wave a magic wand and make that go away, I would. No, the bad thing is the other part of my job."

"Which is?" I said, curious.

"The part where I get you to think about the most important thing in your life: yourself."

"Oh brother," I said, "you're starting to sound like one of those cheesy self-help books. 'You need to take a swim in Lake You.' 'You've built yourself an emotional prison and it's time to fire the warden.' Yuck!"

"I'm not so sure," he said. "Cheesiness aside, there is validity to those comments. We do need to be introspective, swim in our own lakes to better understand what makes us tick. And as for emotional prisons and wardens … so often I have patients come in here, troubled by some event in their past that they are convinced still defines their present. But that's not true—the only thing that defines your present is what your present self thinks. The past is dead. Gone. And sometimes you just have to move on."

"What if you can't?" I thought about my three hundred years of vampireyness and how much pain and death I had caused during those years. The thought of just letting it go and moving on felt like I would be taking the easy, selfish path.

I didn't think any of that out loud, but this astute man must have gathered a general understanding of my resistance because he said, "I'm not telling you to forget your past, especially if you have something to make up for. I'm just saying that guilt and purpose are two different things. Guilt is the unconstructive punishment we self-inflict in some vain attempt to fix what was done. That's useless. Purposeful action as an answer to the sins of our past … that's something else. But purposeful action is only effective if we are our whole selves—clear-thinking, determined, strong. That's the only way you can truly make up for the bad you've done."

He put down his notebook and pen before leaning in close. "But so many of us don't let go of the guilt because we don't feel that we deserve to be whole. And there's the rub: do you feel you deserve to be whole as you try to make up for what you've done, or do you feel that the emptiness you described to me is part of the punishment you believe you deserve?"

There are moments when my own emotions have surprised me. Moments when I have reacted to something said or done before I even knew what I was doing.

Hearing those words invoked one of those moments for me, and I did something I hadn't done since I was made human again all those weeks ago.

I smiled.

↔

No cookie-cutter solutions. He was right about that.

But he was also wrong about a lot of things when it came to me. Truth was, there was no way for him to get it right, as I hadn't told him nearly enough. But I knew. And what he said rang true: if I had a chance to make up for a fraction of the pain I'd caused, I needed a clear head, and I needed a strong will.

There's the rub, indeed. I knew what I needed to do to be myself again, but refused to believe it because I thought I deserved to feel this way.

But if I was going to make up for all the terrible things I'd done, I needed to be myself.

Sure, there were no cookie-cutter solutions, but there was a difference between myself and others who were struggling with these kinds of feelings: I could finally admit what was causing mine.

At least, I could now.

Which meant that I had an advantage. I knew how to fix myself. And after speaking to Ankou, there was no more ambiguity or doubt as to what had happened to me.

My soul was missing.

Leaving the counselor's office for what I hoped would be the last time, I thought about Sonia and her family. Nine lives ruined by something they had lost and could never get back. Nine lives destroyed because they couldn't move on. Nine lives broken because their despair was greater than their will to live.

I couldn't blame them. Fae love is so complete that it is practically physically impossible for them to heal when that love is lost.

But I'm not fae, and the part of me that was missing wasn't lost. I could find it.

I turned on my heels, no longer going uphill toward my bed and comfort. Instead I went to the Other Studies Library.

Down in the archives, I retrieved the amulet and held it in my hands. I pulled out the radio to contact the raspy man, which crackled with his grating voice. "Katri—"

"You said our souls are trapped together. You said that you can feel me, feel when I do something that saddens or excites my soul. Tell me, can you feel this?"

I shut off the radio, and holding the amulet with both hands, I formulated my question within me. When I felt those words with all my being, I uttered them out loud.

"Where am I?" I said, and every fiber of my being knew exactly what I meant. Where am I? Where is the part of me that makes me, *me*? Where is my soul?

As the words left my lips, hope filled me. Hope that I'd find myself again. Hope that I would be whole again.

At first nothing happened, and I feared I'd asked the question wrong. Or worse, it wasn't the question I most desired to know the answer to.

A sense of despair grew in me, and just as hope had begun to exit stage left, a pattern started drawing itself on my left arm. The pattern filled itself—a tattoo of light brown and orange and green lines—and I began to understand what was happening.

As the pattern grew, the radio started to crackle. I guessed the raspy man was right … he really could feel my soul, and right now my soul was probably buzzing with excitement as the lights started to form a pattern.

My arm wasn't just my arm anymore.

It was a map. In the center, near the wrist, a glowing red dot.

I looked closer at the map, trying to figure out where that dot was. It took me a few seconds to place the archipelago shape before I realized where it was telling me to go.

"Oh yay," I muttered with a groan, "I guess I'm going to Japan."

ALSO BY RAMY VANCE

Looking for a great deal? Grab these book bundles...

ALSO BY RAMY VANCE

Mortality Bites Series

Mortality Bites

Family Matters

Superhero Me!

Orphaned Follies

Dawn of a Thousand Sunsets

Three Dead Gods

Run, Kat, Run

Encantado Dreams

The Heaviest of Burdens

Shattered Vows

GoneGod World Series

GoneGod World

Keep Evolving

CrystalDreams

Penemue's Inferno

Looking for a great deal? Grab these book bundles...

Setting Fires with Dragons - complete series

Mortality Bites - complete series

Mortality Bound - Complete series

Series Starter - Bundle